The MAN in the PHOTO

A Flagstaff Mystery

DEBBY ARTHUR WARNER

DISCLAIMER

The Man in the Photo: A Flagstaff Mystery is a work of fiction, and all characters depicted are created strictly from the imagination of the author. Any similarities are purely coincidental.

ISBN: 978-1-7349415-1-7

Library of Congress Control Number: 2022903336

First edition
Printed in the United States of America

Cover and text design by Laurie Goralka Design

For more information:
gjauthor@gmail.com
www.debbyarthurwarner.com

Dear Verl—my friend, my love, my support.

To write this book without you was unimaginable,

but your presence was with me,

and I accomplished the unimaginable.

I am forever grateful for the time we had together,

and for your encouraging nature.

You are missed

Acknowledgements

As a writer, I'm very fortunate to have supportive friends who enjoy being on this journey with me. If you've read my other books, you've seen their names before: They are the most loyal, the ones who keep me focused.

After my husband lost his battle with cancer, I had no desire to write. Losing him was difficult in itself, but managing my grief through the months of Covid was unbearable at times. I missed the visits and hugs; I longed to be with family and friends. Entertaining the idea of writing another novel was not something I considered. If it wasn't for my dear friend, Terry Pickens, her daily phone calls during my grieving, and her insistence that I take a Zoom semester class with her—Women Writing for a Change—this book may not have been written.

When we were able to meet again in person, my friends—Terry and Patricia Amadeo—and I would get together weekly, which provided an opportunity for me to share a chapter or two of my newly—but not edited—written work. They caught the obvious misspelled word, forgotten comma, and left-off quotation marks, just to name a few.

Having friends who anxiously look forward to hearing new developments within your story is immeasurable. Nona and Corky Backlund regularly encouraged me to hurry and complete chapters so they could keep up with the characters. Corky even bribed me with his famous Swedish crêpes.

My circle of five confidants included four friends, Terry, Patricia, Nona, and Corky—and my daughter, Leigh Nicks. Leigh called every Saturday morning to get her weekly update.

A few years ago while on a cruise, I met Jimmy and Virginia Parker from Mississippi. Cruising is a great way to meet different and interesting people. We became friends and have cruised together since. Jimmy is a retired police sergeant and a retired deputy sheriff. Thank you, Jimmy, for providing clarity on police procedures when I needed it.

With great appreciation and gratitude, I thank my content editor, Carole London; copy editor, Bonnie Beach; proof-reader, Donna Bettencourt; and graphic designer, Laurie Casselberry. Without them, my work wouldn't be complete.

Chapter One

Driving into the parking lot, Kim passed Sara's car and pulled up in front of the Unique Boutique. Kim was proud of her daughter and what she had accomplished in just a few years. After her father died from pancreatic cancer four years earlier, Sara wanted to do something meaningful with the money he'd left her. She'd always wanted to open a clothing boutique second to none, and she did. She knew her father would be pleased. Sara didn't buy her inventory from the masses: She bought from cottage industries, from women who made each garment individually, and no two pieces were exactly alike. Some items could be a little pricey, but her customers didn't mind. They loved the quality and uniqueness of each piece. And they loved Sara, she was always pleasant and helpful. The boutique was in a strip mall south of Flagstaff just outside of town and not too far from where Sara lived.

Before getting out of the car, Kim noticed the lights inside the boutique weren't on. She knew Sara was there because she'd seen her car, and she knew her daughter's routine. Sara always came in through the back of the store and walked through the small office space into the main area. She'd set her purse and keys by the register and immediately turn on the lights before putting the purse and keys in the storage closet. The money pouch was emptied into the register and placed in the drawer until closing time, when she'd fill it back up to take home. Sara had planned to open up thirty minutes earlier that morning so her mother could shop for a dress before customers arrived. Her car was there, but where was Sara?

For a few seconds, Kim just sat staring in the shop windows, waiting for the lights to come on. She looked at her watch: It was 9:15. Sara had had plenty of time to get inside and turn on the lights. Kim wondered if there had been a power outage, but the traffic lights were working, the gas station on the corner had lights, and even the shoe store and bakery in the strip mall had their lights on. Kim was beginning to feel anxious. She jumped out of the car and rushed to the front door, but when she tried to open it, it was locked. She peered in the window, but there was no sign of Sara. She walked around to the back of the store in hopes of finding her there with someone. She wasn't there. Kim tried the back door, but it was also locked, and then she remembered that the back door, when closed, automatically locked on the outside as a safety feature. She pounded on it, but to no avail. Where was Sara? She checked her surroundings hoping to see someone who might have seen Sara, but there was no one in sight.

Now it was 9:30 and the rest of the stores were opening. She ran to the closest store to Sara's, which was the shoe shop, and frantically pushed the door open. She recognized the shop owner, Ron. She'd bought a pair of shoes from him a few months back, and when he realized she was Sara's mother, he couldn't do enough for her. Kim always thought he had a crush on Sara, but she didn't think of Ron that way. She enjoyed talking to him and shopping at his store, but that was all the interest she had.

"Have you seen Sara?" Kim asked.

"Not this morning," he replied. "You're Kim, Sara's mother, right? Nice to see you again. I saw Sara when she left last night and she told me that you were coming early this morning to buy a dress for a dinner party. Why did you ask me if I had seen her? Wasn't she to meet you at nine?"

"Yes, and that's the problem. Sara's not there. Her car's in the parking lot, but she's nowhere to be found. Ron, do you have the phone number for the landlord of the complex? I need to call him and have him open Sara's door. She may have fallen and might be hurt."

"I have his number, I'll get it for you, but I don't think you'll get hold of him right away. He seems to be gone a lot between his travels and other business ventures. You can leave a message and he'll return your call, but it could be hours from now. I suggest you call 911," he said with a concerned look in his eye.

Before calling 911 Kim tried the door again, but it was still locked and the lights were still off. She reached for her phone.

"911, what's your emergency?" Just hearing those words sent shivers through Kim's entire body. "Emergency" conjured up all kinds of unpleasant thoughts—accidents, home invasions, domestic violence and, worse yet, murder. She finally found her voice and explained everything to the dispatcher. Then she remembered that when Sara bought her new car last year, she told Kim that she wanted to leave spare keys to her car, apartment, and the boutique at Kim's house in her childhood bedroom in the dresser drawer in case she ever misplaced one or lost it. She told the dispatcher that she was going home to get the spare key and asked if an officer could meet her at the boutique.

When Kim returned, she saw not one, but two officers standing at the entrance to Sara's place, one male, one female. Kim felt herself shaking. This was all too surreal. Sara was Kim's only child and since Kim's husband passed away, Sara had become her life. What happened to her? Where was she? Kim got out of the car and frantically introduced herself to the officers, letting them know that she was Sara's mother. Officer Beth Clark could see how distraught she was. "Hi, Kim, I'm Officer Clark. I see how worried you are, and understandably so, but maybe there's a good explanation for why she's not here. Maybe her car broke down, or she's stuck in traffic," she said trying to console her.

Kim shook her head. "No, I know that didn't happen. Her car is here in the parking lot."

"Why don't you give me the key to the store and I'll open the door for you," said Officer Clark. Kim readily gave the key to her and nervously waited as the officer opened the door. "My partner, officer Tom Mackey, and I will go in first."

"I'm going in with you," Kim stated.

"Okay, but please stay a few feet behind us so we can secure the area and make sure it's safe."

Upon entering, everything seemed normal until they got to the counter. Kim noticed that Sara's keys and purse were sitting next to the register. So where was Sara? She explained her daughter's routine to the officers and mentioned that after the lights were turned on, Sara would then put her purse and keys in the storage closet.

"Where's the storage closet?" asked Officer Mackey.

"Behind this wall, next to her office space," Kim replied.

"You stay here with Officer Clark while I check the back of the store and the storage closet."

Kim did as she was told, too afraid to see what might be back there. Officer Clark put gloves on and checked around the counter and the drawers, and then opened the drawer to the register. It was empty and the money pouch was nowhere in sight. She made a note of it. Kim was watching her every move. "Officer Clark, the register is empty and the money pouch isn't here, so what does that mean?"

"I'm not sure. Someone could have seen her enter with the money pouch, followed her in, grabbed the pouch, and ran. Sara may have chased after him, and she still might be out there looking for him and just hasn't gotten back yet." That thought gave Kim a little hope until she realized how much time had passed. She knew Sara wouldn't still be out there chasing a thief.

Meanwhile, Officer Mackey looked around the small office space, but nothing seemed disturbed. The computer on the desk was still closed, indicating it hadn't been turned on yet. There were some notes and a few receipts stacked neatly on the left side of the desk. It didn't appear there was a struggle, and the back door showed no signs of forced entry. He opened the door to the storage closet. There were shelves on both sides with boxes neatly stacked, which he assumed was inventory. He scratched his head, perplexed as to what might have happened in the boutique that morning. Realizing Sara could have been kidnapped—and at gunpoint, since there was no sign of a struggle, he called the precinct and asked for a detective to come out.

When Officer Mackey returned to the front room, Officer Clark told him about the money pouch and the register being empty, but otherwise she found nothing suspicious. "Same here," he said. "No sign of foul play. Everything was orderly and in its place. I called in for a detective who should be here shortly." He looked at Kim, aware she was listening to every word, and tried to reassure her that everything possible would be done to find Sara. He refrained from telling her that Sara might have been kidnapped. He encouraged her to go home and wait for news. She refused.

"This is my daughter we're talking about! I'm not going anywhere until I have answers!"

Officer Mackey tried to explain that they may not have any answers right away. "It's a process and could take a while to find out exactly what might have happened to Sara," he said. "Please, there's nothing for you to do here. You'd be better off to go home, gather some pictures of Sara, and wait for a call. Hopefully, she'll call you. We have a detective on the way and he'll want to talk to you, but after that, the best thing for you to do is go home and let us do our job. We'll keep in contact, and you can keep in touch with us."

Kim, realizing she couldn't do anymore, agreed to go home after she talked to the detective. Maybe Sara would show up at her house. It wasn't long before Detective Reynolds appeared. He was tall, mid-fifties, and she could see compassion in his eyes. He introduced himself.

"I know this is a difficult time, but I need to ask you a few questions," he said.

"Okay, but I don't know if I'll have any answers," she said, not sure of the questions.

"When was the last time you talked to Sara?"

"Last night about ten. She called to reassure me that she'd be here promptly at nine this morning."

"How old is Sara?"

"Twenty-nine."

"What does she look like—height, weight, hair color, any noticeable markings such as birthmarks, tattoos, etc.?" Detective Reynolds took the pen off his ear and pulled a small notepad out of his right pocket.

"She's about 5'6" or 5'7". I'm not good with weight, but she's a runner and a little on the thin side. Maybe 125 pounds, if that. Her hair is very short, more like a pixie style combed towards her face. It's dark, not black, kind of a chestnut color. She doesn't have a birthmark and there are no tattoos or body piercings that I know of. In her face, she's a younger-looking version of me, only she's a couple inches taller and several pounds lighter."

"Would you have any idea what she might be wearing?" he asked as he continued to write.

"No. We didn't discuss what she was going to wear today, but I can almost guarantee that she had on a pair of loafers. She has several pairs in different colors and likes to color coordinate with her outfits. She likes loafers for work because they're comfortable. Detective, Sara's car is still in the parking lot, so wherever she is, she didn't take her car."

"I'll walk out with you and you can show me which one it is. Do you have a key for it?"

Kim thought about the three keys she found when she went home to get the key for the boutique. Each key had a tag on it indicating whether it went to the store, car, or her apartment. "I do have a spare to her car, but it's at home. It never occurred to me to bring it when I went to get the key to the store. I can't believe I didn't think of that," she said, upset with herself.

"It's understandable, you had a lot on your mind. We'll eventually get the key, but for now, there are other things I need to know, Mrs.—I'm sorry, I didn't get your last name."

"It's Walker, but please call me Kim." Before the detective could ask his next question, Kim pointed out Sara's white Prius. "This is it," she said. He observed the exceptionally well-kept vehicle and then checked the doors. They were locked as Kim had suspected, telling the detective that Sara was a very cautious person. He looked through the windows of the spotless car, impressed with how clean it was and said as much to Kim. "My daughter likes things to be neat and orderly. Her apartment is just as clean as her car, and everything is in its place."

"Kim, is Sara married, or has she ever been married?"

"No. She's been too busy getting her business up and running. She doesn't feel she has time for a committed relationship right now."

"What about boyfriends, past and present."

"I'd have to think about that. I know there were a few different guys she dated once in a while, but when they started to get serious, she'd quit seeing them. She liked having someone to go to dinner and a movie with and just to hang out with at times, but she always made it clear that she wasn't ready for a serious relationship. If they couldn't accept her terms, she quit seeing them."

"Did she ever mention anyone she dated that might have been extremely upset when she wouldn't see them anymore?"

"Not to my knowledge. Sara was pretty private about her personal life. She said when she was ready for a relationship and found Mr. Right, then she would definitely share that with me."

"What about girlfriends, would she have confided in them?"

"Maybe."

"Just one more question for now and then I'll let you leave, but I would like for you to make a list of names and phone numbers of as many of her friends and acquaintances that you can think of. Anything that you can share with us will be helpful. Kim, do you know of anyone who might want to harm Sara?"

The thought of anyone wanting to hurt Sara unnerved her. Her knees weakened and she leaned against the Prius for support. "No, Detective, everyone liked Sara. She's just one of those people. She's very kind and extremely friendly, and has a personality that won't quit. Never judgmental and accepts everyone for who they are."

"Did she ever talk about a disgruntled customer?"

"No," Kim said, shaking her head. She was still leaning against the car and now the detective was standing in front of her. She looked up into his eyes. "Sara has a lot of repeat business and her customers love her. She never talked about anyone being unhappy with their purchase, and if they were, she would've made it right."

"Thank you, you've been very helpful. I know how scary this must be for you, but try not to worry. Kim, I'll need your address, and I'll stop by later to get a picture of Sara and any other information you might have for me at that time. I'll also get the key to her car, unless it's on her key ring in the store."

"I didn't think about that, it probably is. What about her purse? I know she wouldn't want it left in the store. Can I take it home with me?"

"I'm going to call forensics and have them check for fingerprints, so we'll need to hang on to her belongings until we do that."

"Detective, please tell me you'll find my daughter. Please tell me she'll be okay," Kim pleaded. But now when she looked into his eyes, she saw more than compassion: She saw concern.

Chapter Two

The forensic technicians finished up, but the report from the department head was disappointing. "Sorry, Detective," said Ben, delivering the discouraging news, "but we couldn't get a clear, distinguishable fingerprint anywhere, except for two on the back doorknob and a few on the purse, which were probably put there by the owner. We'll compare them and let you know what we find out, but I'm sure they're the same. What I find strange is that her purse doesn't seem to have been touched after she set it on the counter. Her wallet, driver's license, money and credit cards are still in the purse. We didn't find a cell phone."

"That's actually encouraging," said Detective Reynolds. "If she has her cell phone with her, then maybe she'll have an opportunity to call. If she was kidnapped and her wallet and keys weren't touched, then whoever took her acted quickly, probably when she went to turn on the lights. I'll call her mother and ask her to meet me at Sara's apartment. Maybe we can find something there that will give us a clue as to what happened."

Kim arrived before Detective Reynolds. She thought about waiting in the car for him but decided to wait in Sara's apartment instead. She hoped against hope that she'd find

Sara there, but at the same time she was concerned about what she'd find if she was there. Anxious, but also hesitant, she slowly unlocked the door.

Sara's apartment was open concept. At the entry, the living room was to the right and the kitchen and dining area to the left. Above the sink was a large bay window. The sun was shining in, casting light throughout the room. The apartment felt empty. Kim stood still in the quietness, observing how untouched everything looked. There wasn't a dirty dish anywhere, not even a morning coffee cup. As clean and orderly as Sara was, if she was rushed in the morning, she'd often leave her cereal bowl and coffee cup in the sink to be dealt with when she returned home. She was a creature of habit and loved Starbucks, but she was disciplined enough to only allow her indulgence twice a week. Kim wasn't sure which days Sara went there, so it was possible she might have gone that morning. She made a mental note to tell Detective Reynolds, just in case someone followed her from Starbucks to the boutique.

Leaving the door open for the detective, Kim started down the short hallway to Sara's bedroom, still holding her purse and a folder with information to give him. She'd only gotten a couple of steps when she heard him come in.

"Sorry I'm a few minutes late. I didn't get away as quickly as I'd intended." He looked at the folder. "Is that for me?" he asked. Before Kim could answer, she got a beep on her phone indicating she had a new text. She glanced at it and immediately backed up to the sofa and sat down. "What is it, Kim?"

"It's a text from Sara." She read it out loud.

"Hi, Mom. I know this is late notice, but it was a spur-of-the-moment decision. One of my friends, I don't believe you've met her yet, called me last night with an offer I couldn't refuse. I'll explain more later. . . after all, this is a text, but I wanted to let you know that I'll be gone about a week to ten days. Love you, Sara."

Kim dropped the phone in her lap and began to cry. Detective Reynolds sat down next to her. "You don't believe that was from Sara, do you?"

"I *know* that wasn't from Sara. She never would have done that, especially since we were going to meet this morning. She would've called or left me a text message even if it was the middle of the night. She knows how I worry. And, it couldn't have been her, because she'd never have left her car in the mall parking lot, or her purse and keys in the boutique."

"I know," he said. "That's the first thing I thought of when you were reading it. Kim, I know how upsetting this is, but let's work it to our advantage. After I look through the apartment and check for any possible clues, I want you to answer that text as if you believe it is from Sara. We need to buy time."

"But what will I say?"

"I'll tell you what to say. I'll also need Sara's cell number so we can get her phone records. We'll check to see who she's talked to recently and see if we can get a location of where this text message came from. But right now, I want to check the other rooms."

Entering Sara's bedroom, everything looked normal, even the bathroom. Then they went into the second bedroom that Sara used as her study and home office. Against the wall was a small hide-a-bed that could be used for an occasional overnight guest. Nothing was out of place and nothing appeared questionable until Detective Reynolds opened the large calendar on Sara's desk. From January through March, she'd written down appointments with doctors, her dentist, an eye exam, a few dinners, outings with friends, and when to expect a delivery for something she'd purchased online. But when he got to the present month—April—he noticed the days leading up to April 22, had several notations on them, almost like a diary entry.

April 6: she wrote: "Today marks the third time I got a hang-up call, but this time they didn't hang up until I asked 'who is this?'"

April 8: "Hang-up call, music playing in background. Calls always in morning or early evening when I'm at home."

April 11: "Didn't hear anything for 3 days, thought the calls had stopped. Then, first time got call while at Boutique. Didn't answer. Voicemail, heavy breathing. Unknown caller, no number."

April 12: "Called Kristy, told her about calls."

Detective Reynolds looked at Kim. "Who's Kristy?"

"She's Sara's best friend. They've known each other since childhood."

"Have you talked to her lately?"

"Yes, today. I called her as soon as I got home from the boutique. I asked if she'd heard from Sara. She said the last time she'd spoken with her was yesterday on her lunch hour. I told her what was going on. She tried not to sound worried and reminded me just how resilient and strong Sara is, mentally and physically. Since Sara lived alone, she'd taken a self-defense course, and a few months ago she enrolled in a martial art's class. She really enjoys it and goes every week on Saturday morning."

"I'll need Kristy's phone number, if you have it."

"Just a minute," Kim said, and went to get the folder. "It's in here." She handed it to him and he opened it while sitting at Sara's desk, dumping the contents out. There were two sheets of paper with names and phone numbers and three photos of Sara.

Detective Reynolds studied the pictures. "She looks exactly the way you described her to me. This will be very helpful." He picked up the papers. Some of the names had addresses with phone numbers by them and others didn't.

"Detective, this is all the information I could find. I put an asterisk by those that I know are her friends. I met a few of them when Sara brought me along with her to some of their cookouts. I think Kristy will be a lot more help to you when you get in touch with her. She told me that as soon as we hung up, she was going to call some of their mutual friends and see if any of them had spoken with Sara since last night."

Detective Reynolds looked back at the calendar. "Kim, did you know about these phone calls?"

"No. She never mentioned them."

April 17: 8 p.m. "Unknown caller, didn't answer. Called every minute until I picked up. Voice said, don't hang up. Music in background. I asked who it was. He said, we'll meet soon. Called Kristy."

April 18: "Called police as Kristy suggested. They can't do anything, caller didn't threaten me. If calls persist and become more intense, could monitor my phone. I'll think about that."

April 21: "Unknown caller, 6:30 a.m. didn't answer. Calls continue. 7 a.m. frustrated, answered, yelled in phone—leave me alone! Caller, 'I've been watching you. Soon we'll meet' . . . click."

April 22: "Meet mom 9 a.m. Go to police station first, request phone be monitored."

Kim, reading this along with the detective, moved to the hide-a-bed and sat down. The full impact of what was happening finally registered. "Oh, my gosh! Someone's taken Sara! Why didn't she tell me about these calls? If I'd known, there might have been something I could've done. Detective, Sara's been kidnapped! We have to find her before he hurts her!" Kim broke down and cried into her hands.

"Kim, we will," he said trying to reassure her, "but the best thing you can do for Sara right now is to try and stay calm. Let's begin by answering her text. We want the sender to think that you believe the message is from Sara. Take a deep breath, get your phone, and let's do this."

Chapter Three

Sara arrived at the boutique ten minutes early so she could be ready for her mother when she got there. She knew her mom's taste in clothing and wanted to have a few items set aside to try on when she arrived. She parked in her favorite spot in the front parking lot because the lighting was better than the lot in the back, but she always entered the boutique from the back door. She used to enter through the front until, on several occasions, she encountered early customers who wanted to enter the boutique with her. To avoid the unpleasantries of having to tell them they would need to wait until the store officially opened, it was easier to just enter from the back.

Sara had planned to stop by the police station before going to the boutique, but she was concerned it could take longer than she anticipated and didn't want to be late for her mother, and then have to explain why. She knew how worried her mother would be if she found out about the phone calls. She decided to call instead and made arrangements to see an officer the next morning.

After setting her purse and keys on the counter, Sara went to turn the lights on when she saw a man at the front door. She paused, hoping he'd leave, but he peered in and began to knock. Still holding the money bag under her arm, she walked over and pointed to the sign, indicating she wasn't open yet. He pulled a badge from his pocket and held it up for her to see. He wasn't wearing a police uniform so she didn't realize that he was a cop.

Sara opened the door and asked, "Are you the officer I spoke with on the phone this morning?"

"No, but I heard about your call and wanted to come by and talk with you."

"I don't have time to talk with you now. When I called this morning, I said I'd stop in tomorrow morning, and I prefer to do it then. My mother will be here any minute now and I don't want her to know about the calls—at least not yet, not until I can reassure her that the situation is under control."

He ignored her request and boldly walked in. "This will only take a minute, and if she comes while I'm here, you can tell her I'm a salesman," he said with a tone of authority. Reluctantly, she agreed and then relocked the door.

Still holding the money bag under her arm, she suggested they talk in her office. If her mother arrived while he was still there, then he could leave through the back. Sara led the way, but once they were in the office area and out of public view, she felt an object pressed firmly against her back.

"Don't move a muscle," he ordered. "I have a gun, and if you do anything stupid, I won't hesitate to use it."

Sara, thinking she was being robbed, offered up the money bag. "If it's money you want, it's all in here. Please take it and go," she pleaded.

"I'll take the money, it might come in handy, but that's not why I'm here."

"Then why are you here?" she asked, realizing that this could be the person who'd been tormenting her with those harassing phone calls. After all, she thought, he did say he was watching her and they would meet soon.

"I'm here for *you*."

"What do you want with me?"

"Don't concern yourself with that. If you do what I say, you'll be safe. Don't try to yell or do anything funny, just walk out the back door and over to the big white van."

Sara knew that if she got into his van, she might not make it back alive. She thought about her self-defense and martial arts training and wondered if she could successfully use a technique she'd learned. But knowing there was a gun at her back, she wasn't comfortable with her options. Either way, she knew once she left that room, she might die. She had to try something. With all her strength, she quickly flung her leg around and tried to kick the gun out of his hand. He grabbed her foot, knocked her to the floor, and pointed the gun at her head.

"That was stupid! Don't try that again or you won't make it through another day. And just so you know, I hold five black belts. I'm not a novice like you, so don't think you can outmaneuver me."

Sara laid there, staring up at him and studying his face. He had a large blue cap pulled down over his forehead. She could hardly see his eyes, but there was something vaguely familiar about him. She felt she had seen him before, but she couldn't recall where. While he towered over her in his tight polo shirt, she could see how muscular he was, and it became obvious that she was no match for him.

Still pointing the gun at her head, he took the money pouch, pulled the gun to his side, and placed the money pouch over it, rendering it less noticeable. He backed away from Sara, then told her to get up slowly and walk out the back door as if nothing was wrong.

"If you try to pull something, you're dead! I have nothing to lose."

Sara, understanding her limitations, did as she was told. As she walked out the back door, she was hopeful someone might see her and find it strange that she'd be getting in a van and leaving her boutique that time of morning. It was quiet outside, and since it was still early, she didn't see anyone in either direction. She walked to the white van and waited for further instructions. She was told to open the back side door on the passenger side, get in, and put on the seatbelt. He opened the front door, set the money pouch down, picked up a roll of duct tape, and tore off a large piece. He stuck the gun under his arm and told Sara to put her arms together. He wrapped the tape around her wrists as tight as he could, then he secured her feet. Lastly, he put tape over her mouth and eyes. There were no windows in the back of the van for anyone to see that she was being held against her will, so she didn't understand why he had to tape her eyes. Then it registered: He didn't want her to know where they were going.

As the van drove off, Sara was overwhelmed with a sense of impending doom.

Chapter Four

Detective Reynolds was fixated on Sara's calendar when Officer Mackey walked in his office.

"Detective, Kent just stopped by my desk and told me about a phone call that came in this morning," said Officer Mackey. "He heard Sara Walker was missing and he said she called this morning about 8:30 wanting to know if someone would be available to talk with her early tomorrow. She told him she'd been getting harassing phone calls, they were becoming more aggressive, and she was frightened."

Detective Reynolds glanced at the calendar again. "According to her calendar, she was planning on coming in this morning. I checked with Steve at the front desk and he said no one by that name had stopped by. He obviously didn't know she'd called. Tom, get the word out that any information coming into this department pertaining to Sara Walker gets put on my desk. I know we're shorthanded right now, and Jack won't be back for a couple more weeks, but I could sure use some help." He looked straight in Tom Mackey's eyes when he said, "I'm afraid if we don't find Sara soon, we may be looking for her *body* instead."

Mackey nodded his head. "I know time is of the essence, but we should be getting her phone records soon, and hopefully that will give some clues. At least we should find out who's been making those calls."

Detective Luke Reynolds liked and appreciated Officer Tom Mackey. He knew he'd make detective one day, but right now he needed his partner Jack on this case. He and Jack had been partners for the last ten years, and they could almost read each other's thoughts. Luke had never worked alongside anyone he enjoyed more than Jack. Unfortunately, his partner was on sick leave, recovering from rotator cuff surgery.

"Tom, I'm headed over to the mall to view footage from their security cameras. You want to come along?"

"You mean you finally got ahold of the landlord?"

"Yeah, I'm to meet him," Luke looked down at his watch, "in fifteen minutes. You coming?"

"Yes *sir*," he said emphatically, pleased to be asked.

On the drive over, Luke thought about the text he had Kim send to Sara's phone. He told her to tell Sara that she was surprised she left without telling her, but to have a good time and take lots of pictures. She asked Sara to call as soon as she could because she had some very important news to tell her. And then added, "I know how you hate waiting to hear anything, so I'm sure I'll hear from you before the end of the day." The detective wanted the kidnapper to feel he'd convinced Kim that the text he'd sent indeed came from Sara. He didn't want him to suspect anything. He also wanted whoever sent the text to know that Kim would be expecting a response. Luke needed to keep him engaged if there was any hope of finding Sara.

The mall manager, Jess Higgins, was very cooperative and had everything set up for the detective and Mackey when they arrived. Detective Reynolds asked to view the front cameras first. At exactly 8:55 a.m., they see a figure walk up to Sara's boutique. The cameras were old and the film was grainy, but they could tell by his physique that it was a man. Soon, the door opened and the man went inside and out of sight.

"I need you to back it up," said the detective. "Start from where the camera first picks him up. I want to see if it shows him getting out of his vehicle."

"I'll try," said Higgins, "but I haven't had a need to review these tapes before, and I'm not sure exactly how all this works. We'll probably have to repeat the process several times in order to get to the point you're wanting to see."

"You're doing fine, and I appreciate your help. We'll need to borrow the tapes and let our experts view them. They might be able to enlarge the picture and enhance the quality, but right now I can't waste time taking them to the department first. I'm working against the clock, and I need any and all information as quickly as I can get it. Hopefully I'll find out something before I leave here."

After reviewing the footage several times, it was clear that the man came from around the corner of the building and not from the parking lot. Detective Reynolds asked to see the video from the back of the building. It was a little clearer, but not much. It wasn't long before they saw Sara and the man coming out the back door. The back cameras didn't have the range like the front cameras and only showed them walking until they were out of sight. It never showed Sara getting in the white van or being duct taped. Their hopes dwindled. The detective asked Higgins to zoom in on Sara and the man, who appeared to have something under his arm by his side. Sara was walking stoically ahead of him.

"Thanks, Mr. Higgins. We appreciate your time and patience," said Detective Reynolds. "The department will return the videos as soon as we're through with them."

"I'm glad I could be of help, Detective. I'm sorry the results weren't more productive."

"Maybe our experts can pull up more than we've been able to identify at this time." Luke replied, then turned to Officer Mackey, "Mackey, let's walk the back parking lot and see if we can find anything."

They combed the area several times but found nothing. The detective was becoming more concerned. Finding Sara was going to be as difficult as finding a needle in a haystack. At this point, they had nothing to go on. Hopefully Sara's phone records would show something. He was anxious to get back to the precinct. If the same number showed up on the days marked on her calendar, then he might learn the identity of the kidnapper.

When they returned to the precinct, Officer Beth Clark was the first to approach them. "Detective, you're not going to like this, but I have discouraging news," she said.

"What now?" he asked.

"We have Sara's phone records, and the unfamiliar number that called on the days she recorded on her calendar can't be linked to anyone. It appears the caller used a burner phone. There's no record of who, or where, those calls came from. I'm sorry, Detective, I know this isn't what you wanted to hear."

The detective looked defeated. "I don't know how I'm going to explain this to her mother. It's as though she vanished without a trace. We have no clues; he hasn't answered the text Kim sent or she would've called me. The day isn't over so hopefully she'll hear something. Beth, I want to go over the phone records. I want to see who she's been talking to in the last few weeks."

"I knew you would. They're on your desk," she said. "Oh, one more thing: The last ping on Sara's phone from the cell towers was just this side of the Arizona-Utah border. Her phone went quiet after that."

"He's taking her out of our jurisdiction and above what we're capable of doing without more help. We might need to get the FBI involved, and there's one other person who could be more help than anyone. I just hope he's available. Here, Beth," he handed her the tapes, "get these in the right hands. I'll be in my office."

Chapter Five

The officers piled in the briefing room as requested by Detective Reynolds. Once everyone assembled, he went over the limited information he had on Sara Walker and asked each officer to be alert to anyone or anything suspicious. He handed them a photo of Sara and then showed the video footage from the mall.

"As you can see, we have little to go on. The video has been enhanced, ever so slightly, but just enough to estimate the kidnapper's height at approximately six feet, given the fact that Sara is about 5'6" or 5'7," The detective zoomed in on the male figure. He noted that the suspect could either be Caucasian or Latino. "It appears he has a large tattoo on his right arm," he continued. "If you look closely, you can almost make out a broken heart with a snake going through where the heart breaks. This may or may not be relevant to something that occurred in his personal life. Unfortunately, his face is harder to make out because his cap conceals most of it, and he's not facing the camera. I need all of you to make a mental note of the tattoo. It may come in handy." Detective Reynolds looked around the room. "Thompson, I want you to check out every convenience store in the area and ask if anyone's seen a tattoo like this. Mackey and Hampson, see if the gas station across from the strip mall has security cameras that might've picked up a vehicle leaving from the back. Also, check on any homes in the area that have cameras. There has to be a camera somewhere that captures a vehicle during that time of the morning. Clark has already left to talk with the business owners in the mall, then she'll check out tattoo parlors and see if any of the artists have done a tattoo like this. I'm headed over to Starbucks to see if Sara was there this morning, and then I'm going to meet with her friend, Kristy. Thompson, Mackey and Hampson—call me immediately if you come across anything. The rest of you, pay attention to any unusual activity."

On his way out the door, Detective Luke Reynolds stopped by his desk to get the folder with the names and addresses that Kim had given him. He was hopeful he'd get more information from Kristy before interviewing the list of friends and acquaintances. Just as he approached the car his cell rang.

"Hello?"

"Detective Reynolds, this is Kim Walker. I just got a text. You told me to call as soon as I did."

"Yes, Kim, I want to be notified whenever there's communication from Sara's phone." He could tell by the tone in her voice that she was very concerned. "I'm guessing it wasn't from Sara."

"Not only that, it wasn't even from Sara's phone," she said, her voice shaking.

"What do you mean? What did it say?"

"It said that she lost her phone while she and her friend were on a rollercoaster and she wanted to wait until she was back home to replace it. In the meantime, she picked up a cheap disposable one that she said would do for now, because she didn't care to get texts or phone calls while she was gone. And as far as the important news I had, well . . . if I couldn't text it, then she'd wait to find out when she returned. Detective, I'm scared. If whoever took her, and got rid of her phone, will he do the same to her?"

Damn! the detective thought. *Another burner phone.* "Kim, I know you're frightened, but as long as he stays in touch, there's hope, and it gives us time to find her."

"Should I answer him?"

"Yes, but not right away. Let him wait a while and wonder what you're thinking. I'll call you later, but first, there's someone I want to talk to before you respond. He's someone I have a lot of confidence in, someone who recently worked on a kidnapping case which was solved with positive results."

"Detective, I had flyers printed, and some of my friends are coming over to help me distribute them."

The detective thought about flyers being posted everywhere, and he wasn't comfortable with Kim doing that just yet. "I know that seems like the most reasonable thing to do, Kim, but I want you to wait, at least until tomorrow. We don't know what this is all about yet. If something happened to Sara, I don't think he'd still be communicating with you. He thinks you believe the texts are from her. If he gets wind of the flyers and realizes you know she's been taken, all correspondence will stop. It may put Sara in a more dangerous situation." Detective Reynolds was beginning to believe that the kidnapper might be right under his nose. He probably knew the police would check her phone records, and they would know from the cell towers where her last location was. He could have driven to the state line just to throw them off and probably ditched her phone there.

"Detective, I'm going crazy with worry. I *have* to do something."

"I know it's hard, but hold tight a little longer. I have officers working in different directions, and hopefully I'll have more information by the end of the day. If the media gets on this before we're ready, all hell could break loose." Before the detective could finish, his phone beeped. "Kim, hold on a minute, I have a call coming in." He saw it was Tom Mackey.

"Mackey, you got something?"

"We might have gotten our first lucky break," Mackey said. "The surveillance camera from the service station showed a white van leaving from the back parking lot of the strip mall shortly after Sara and the suspect left her boutique. And get this—no other vehicle was seen leaving the parking lot within ten minutes from when they did. It's got to be them," said Officer Mackey.

"Did you get the license number?"

"No, it was too blurry. But we do know that it's a Ford Econoline and looks to be between a 2010 to 2014 model. Hampson and I are headed back to the department. We'll pull up every vehicle within a twenty-five mile radius that fits the description, and hopefully we can narrow the search to a specific year."

"Thanks, Mackey. We now have something to go on. I'm headed to Starbucks. I'll ask if anyone has seen a van like that in the area." Luke was encouraged by the news and almost forgot he had Kim waiting.

"Sorry to keep you on hold, Kim. I don't want to give you false hope, but we might have a legitimate lead. Do you know anyone who drives a white van?"

Chapter Six

Luke Reynolds had heard many stories about private investigator Joe Conrad from Luke's, uncle, Dan Mathews. Joe, on occasion—as did Luke—used Dan's resources when he needed help solving a difficult case. Dan's agency specialized in background investigative research and Joe mainly used them when he didn't have time to do the work himself. Dan had told Luke about the kidnapping of a prominent family's child and how Joe was instrumental in rescuing the child and bringing him home unharmed. Long before Dan retired and turned the agency over to Joe, Luke stopped by to return something to Dan and Joe was there. That was the only time he'd met Joe, but he liked him immediately. When Dan decided to retire, he told Luke that if he ever needed or wanted help, or someone just to talk over a troubling case with, Joe Conrad would be the person to contact. It was time to call him.

"Conrad Investigative Agency,"

"Is Joe available?"

"May I ask whose calling?" the receptionist asked in a gentle tone as she always did.

"Detective Luke Reynolds, Is he there or not?" Luke said sharply.

"One moment, please, I'll get him for you," she contin-ued in her gentle voice.

Luke was surprised he'd snapped at her, but the day had been trying and his patience was running thin. Before he could apologize, she was gone and replaced by a male voice.

"Hello, Joe here."

"Hey, Joe. This is Luke Reynolds, Dan Mathews' nephew. I don't know if you remember me . . ."

Joe interrupted. "Oh, yeah, I met you at the agency before Dan retired. You came by to return a folder to him. He invited you to go to lunch with us, but you were on your way to interview a witness and asked for a raincheck."

"Geez, now I know why my uncle thought so much of you. You have a memory like an elephant."

Joe laughed. "You're hard to forget when the first twenty minutes of lunch was spent talking about you. It's my understanding that you're Flagstaff's finest." Now he had Luke laughing.

"You can't believe everything my uncle said." Luke changed subjects quickly and got to the point. "Listen, Joe, on a more serious note, there's something I want to discuss with you. I don't know what your schedule's like the next few days, but I have a missing person who we now know has been kidnapped, and I could use your help sooner than later."

"Luke, I know you wouldn't be calling if it wasn't seri-ous. Dan told me you didn't care much for P.I.s except for him. Kelly, my assistant, and I just wrapped up a cold case we'd been working on for the last two months. And thanks to Dan, when he retired and turned the agency over to me, I inherited not only his staff, but a couple of highly qualified investigators. They can handle anything that needs attention. I will make myself available. Tell me about the case.

Luke filled him in on the details and how they were clueless until they got the footage of the white van, but that was all they had to go on. No one at Starbucks had seen the van, and they didn't know anyone who had a tattoo with a snake running through a broken heart. And no one remembered seeing Sara in the last three days. He also told Joe about the texts Kim was getting.

"I think you're right in having Kim respond to the text as if she believes it's Sara. I'd have her keep that up, but when she answers his last text, have her ask again for Sara to call her. If Sara is alive, he may have her call Kim to convince her that she's okay so her mother won't expect any more texts—at least until the seven to ten days are up. It's not ransom he wants or he would've already asked for it. Have you had a chance to talk with any of her friends?"

"Her closest friend, Kristy, is due here in about ten minutes. I was supposed to meet with her earlier at the clinic where she works as a receptionist, but she called and asked if she could stop by here after work so she wouldn't be distracted. I have a list with names of Sara's friends and acquaintances that Kim put together for me, and I'll be reviewing that with Kristy. Hopefully someone will know who drives a white van and has a tattoo. Joe, I know this is short notice, but can you come by here in the morning? I can show you the footage from the security cameras, and Mackey should have the list of registered white Ford vans narrowed down by then."

"I can be there by 8:30. My assistant, Kelly Murphy, will be with me. Once you get to know her, you'll understand how valuable she is and why I seldom work a case without her."

"I gotta go, Joe. Someone is coming my way and it might be Kristy. Thanks for your help. See you in the morning." Just as he hung up, a petite redhead walked into his office. He stood up to greet her. "You must be Kristy," he said, extending his hand. She nodded as they shook hands and sat down in the chair in front of his desk.

"I'm assuming you're Detective Reynolds," she said with a worried look on her face.

"I am. Thank you, Kristy, for coming in. I know this is a difficult time."

"Detective, do you have any idea what might've happened to Sara?"

"We know she's been kidnapped. We're pretty sure the person who took her drives a white van. Kristy, do you know anyone who drives a white van?"

Kristy took a moment before answering. "No, I'm sorry, but no one comes to mind."

"What about a handyman? Has Sara used one recently? Or a delivery service, anyone she could've come in contact with who might drive that type of van?"

"I'm sorry, but I can't think of anyone," said Kristy. Then, almost as if the detective's words just registered, she said, "I can't imagine why or how Sara was kidnapped. She's so good at self-defense. He must've caught her off guard." Detective Reynolds didn't mention that he probably had a gun. Instead, he asked about the phone calls.

"We know Sara told you about the calls she was getting . . ." Kristy jumped in before he could finish.

"If you haven't talked to Sara, how do you know about the calls? I was the only one who knew. She wouldn't even tell her mother."

"She documented the calls on her calendar," said the detective. Kristy's big blue-green eyes filled with tears.

"I told her to go to the police and tell them that he was stalking her, and maybe then they'd do something. If she hadn't waited, she might still be here." The tears let go and rolled down her ivory skin. Detective Reynolds handed her a tissue.

"Can I get you a glass of water?" he offered. She shook her head and dabbed at her eyes. She looked fragile, almost as if she'd break at any moment. Luke realized he'd have to change tactics and get her to talk about their friendship. Maybe she'd remember something that might be useful.

"Kristy, Kim tells me that you've known Sara since childhood."

"Yes. We actually met in kindergarten on the playground. She lived down the street from me, but we didn't know that until we met. We've been like sisters ever since."

"You probably know more about Sara than her mother."

Kristy smiled. "I'm sure there are things Sara told me that she wouldn't tell Kim—especially some of the things we did as teenagers."

"That's what's so great about best friends," said the detective. He looked down on the list of names. "Kristy, I want to ask you about some of the people in Sara's life, her friends and acquaintances, but first, I'd like you to tell me about the men she'd dated in the last few years."

Chapter Seven

They'd been traveling for what seemed like hours before he finally spoke. Sara, relieved he hadn't taped her eyes as tightly as her mouth, tried to look out the small opening at the top, but she couldn't see anything except a little daylight.

"I don't get mean unless someone challenges me," he said. "I want to be nice to you, but that depends on how well you cooperate." Sara tried to respond, but with her mouth taped, all that came out were short mumbling groans. He looked at her through the mirror and pulled over to the side of the road. "I guess I can take the tape off your mouth. We're far enough out in the country that no one would hear you scream—should you be stupid enough to try." He got out of the van, walked over to the back passenger side door, and opened it. He checked to make sure that her ankles and wrists were tightly bound before ripping the tape from her mouth. She gasped when he pulled it off and took a couple of deep breaths. He got back in the van and resumed driving.

Sara wasn't sure exactly how she would talk to him. With nothing to do for hours, she'd given it a lot of thought. She needed to get in his head and try to figure out what kind of person she was dealing with. Now she wished she'd taken more than one semester of psychology. The best chance she had of surviving this ordeal, she told herself, was to choose her words wisely. If he was a sociopath, then trying to reason with him probably wouldn't work; but if he was someone who was going through a mental breakdown due to a divorce, losing his job, financial ruin, or all of the above, her chances were better. She decided to remain silent and wait for him to initiate conversation. All was quiet for about ten minutes.

"For someone who was unable to speak, I thought once I removed the tape, you'd spill your guts." Sara didn't know what his demeanor was like, but his voice sounded steady and calm. She decided to play coy, wanting to give the impression that she wasn't frightened and understood he didn't want to hurt her. She certainly didn't want to challenge him and cause him to become angry.

"I guess I've been waiting for you to tell me why you've taken me. I'm confused. Please tell me why I'm here and where we're going."

"In due time, in due time."

"Do I know you?" He didn't answer. "Have we met before?" she asked, trying not to sound scared, trying to keep her voice even. He remained silent until they turned onto a road that wasn't as smooth as the one they were just on. Sometimes it felt like a bumpy dirt road, but at times, Sara would pick up the sound of gravel. Whatever it was, it was longer than your average driveway.

"Listen and pay attention," he said, "because I'm only going to say this once. When we stop and you get out of the van, you're to do exactly as I say. If you cooperate and don't put up any resistance, I'll be good to you and give you more privileges." Sara was hoping he wouldn't see how scared she was. She listened to his words carefully and considering what he said, she thought maybe his intention wasn't to kill her—at least not right away.

When she was out of the van, he stopped and took the tape off her ankles. Holding on to her arm, he guided her up a few steps and inside a structure. She couldn't tell if it was a house or some other kind of building.

"We'll be going down a flight of stairs. I'll hold your arm as you feel for each step," he told her. When they got to the last step, Sara noticed a damp musty smell, and it felt slightly cooler than it did outside. There was a door at the bottom of the stairs, and once they were inside the room, she heard it close. When they were further in the room, he removed the tape from her eyes but kept her hands bound. She looked around, feeling very uncomfortable with what she saw. It appeared to be a basement. There were no windows, and the floor and walls were concrete. In the back corner was a mattress and a pillow. She noticed a straight-back chair anchored to the floor on the other side of the room. Sara was afraid that her worst fears were about to come true. She was speechless and fought hard to hold back tears. He told her to sit in the chair and he would go over their routine. He stood in front of her and, again, she felt there was something familiar about him. He was still wearing the cap, and she wondered if she'd have that feeling when he removed it. As she sat there waiting for him to speak, she saw a door across from the mattress that she hadn't noticed before.

"That's a bathroom," he said. "It has a toilet, sink, and shower. It also has toilet paper, soap, and a towel. You won't need anything else. I'll bring food and water to you. I want you to like me, Sara. When you get to know me, I think you will. But you need to understand that if you don't respect me or act mean, I'll lock the bathroom door and you won't get fed that day."

Sara's mind was about to explode. She was having a hard time processing what was going on. "Let me get this straight," she said. "You kidnap me, put me in a cellar, threaten to take away bathroom privileges and withhold food, but you want me to *like you*?" Her voice began to escalate. "I don't know who you are. I don't know why I'm here. I don't know how you know me." Once she got started, she couldn't stop. "I was living a happy, normal life until you showed up. You took me at gun point, duct taped me, drove me around for hours, then brought me to this dungeon, and you expect me to like you? Tell me why you're doing this. Tell me you've made a mistake and you're taking me back. Maybe *then* I'll like you."

His face became flushed and he paced back and forth in front of her. His hands were clenched and he started yelling. "Don't act like her, don't act like her! I thought you'd be different, but you're all the same!"

Sara realized what she'd done. She knew she had to do something quickly to calm him down, or there was no telling what would happen. "I *am* different. I'm sorry I upset you. But I'm upset because I don't know what's going on. I don't do well when I don't know." Sara saw his hands begin to open, and then she noticed the tattoo on his arm. "I'm *not* like her. If you'll explain to me why you're doing this, I'll listen and try to understand," she said as calmly as she could. She had to buy time, try not to react, keep him calm, and get him to trust her if she had any hope at all of escaping.

≈ 51 ≈

Chapter Eight

After his conversation with Detective Reynolds, Joe met with Kelly to discuss the kidnapping of Sara Walker.

"I told Luke we'd meet him at 8:30 in the morning. He's going to show us the footage from the surveillance cameras, and anything else he might have by the time we arrive. It's a different case for sure—we have little to go on," Joe told her.

"After we meet with the detective and get what information he has, I'd like to go by the boutique next," said Kelly.

Joe knew, even though Kelly wouldn't admit it, that she wanted to get a sense of the place, a sense of Sara. He noticed, after working with her for the last few months, that she was beginning to listen to, and accept, her intuition. As a former detective, now private investigator, Joe had good instincts, but Kelly had something special, and that's what made them a good team. If they couldn't help solve this case, then it probably wouldn't be solved.

"Joe, in addition to Sara's calendar, the phone calls, her purse and keys left at the boutique, did Luke mention whether anyone had spoken with family members, her friends, or acquaintances?"

"We didn't talk long, but while we were on the phone, Sara's childhood friend was due in at any moment. She showed up, and that ended the call. I'm sure we'll have a better idea of things in the morning."

"Aside from the obvious people to contact, I wonder if Sara kept records with phone numbers of repeat customers. Sometimes small independent shop owners will do that, and it might prove helpful," Kelly said. "And, since it's a boutique for women, I'd like to view the security cameras from the last few weeks to see if a man was frequenting the boutique. I'm sure men have stopped in on occasion to buy a gift for their wives or girlfriends, but if the cameras show the same man several times in the past month, then that would be suspicious."

Joe smiled. "Kelly, how much longer are you going to wait until you get your P.I. license?"

"For the time being, I'm content as your assistant. You never know—one day I might decide to move back to Colorado and work again for the newspaper. I did enjoy being an investigative journalist." Joe shuddered at the idea of not having Kelly around, and he could only hope she was kidding.

"You seriously wouldn't consider that, would you?"

"If you keep bringing up a license I just might," she said with a smile." Getting back to Sara, we'll need to check out her hobbies, activities, if and where she went to church, did she belong to a gym, etc."

"Luke said he was shorthanded, so I don't know how much he'll have accomplished by the time we meet, but I know he can use our help. Once we get the details of whatever they have thus far, then we can better develop our strategy." Kelly didn't respond. Joe could tell she was deep in thought. "Would you like to go out to dinner and toss some ideas around?" he suggested.

Kelly lived 28 miles away in Sedona. It was a slow drive through the narrow, hilly canyon to Flagstaff, which usually took about forty minutes on a good day. Joe lived in Flagstaff not far from the agency. His commute was easy. "Thanks, Joe, but I want to come in the office early tomorrow and go over a few things before we meet with Luke. We've discussed cases over dinner before, and it can last for hours. I don't want to get home too late. I'll take you up on your offer another time."

"You wouldn't have to go home tonight. You can always stay at my place." Kelly shot him a look indicating that that wasn't going to happen. "Don't get the wrong idea. I have a guest room, and that's where I'd expect you to stay."

Kelly laughed. "Well, I'm glad you understand me. And just so you know, I don't keep a toiletry bag and extra set of clothes in my car. But now that I think about it, packing a suitcase and being ready to check into a motel, might not be a bad idea. Until we meet with Luke, we're not sure, exactly, how involved we'll be."

On the drive home, Kelly switched her thoughts from Sara to the complicated relationship she had with Joe. They first met by chance in Cripple Creek, Colorado. Kelly went there searching for answers in the death of her friend, Tara. Joe was in Cripple Creek looking for answers in a murder case he was working. They met when Cripple Creek experienced one of the worst blizzards in years. The roads were closed, and no one could leave for days. When Joe took over Dan Mathews' Agency, he left Colorado Springs and moved to Flagstaff. Kelly had already moved to Sedona by that time. The chemistry between them was getting harder to ignore. She knew Joe felt the same, but he tried to understand her need to keep things between them platonic. *At least he told me he understood,* she thought, *but I know he doesn't think it will interfere with working together like I do. I don't want to chance it and ruin our friendship or our working relationship—at least that's what I keep telling myself,* Kelly's brow furrowed. *Why can't I just accept the obvious? Why do I keep fighting it? Why do I keep asking myself the same questions over and over again? What am I really afraid of? Getting hurt, not having Joe in my life? I would love to move forward with him, but every time I think I can, something holds me back.* Then she smiled, remembering the time Joe kissed her. *We kissed, and I never felt that way with anyone else,* her face softened. *But then I got scared and put the brakes on.* Kelly had been in love before, but the marriage broke up when she realized that he was in love with someone else. Joe was different. Kelly was in love with him, but she was also in denial. *How long will Joe be okay with how things are before he realizes that I'm a dead end and looks elsewhere for someone to share his life with? If that happens it would certainly complicate working together.* Kelly shifted in her seat, uncomfortable with what she was thinking. *Oh, well . . . if it happens, then maybe that's the way it was meant to be and I'll go back to Colorado and work for the* Sentinel. *I can't think about this anymore,* she sighed. *We have a case to solve, and trying to find Sara Walker will take all my energy and keep my mind occupied.*

Chapter Nine

Joe and Kelly arrived promptly at 8:30 the next morning to meet with Detective Reynolds. Joe asked Kelly to wait before getting out of the car, because he had something he wanted to say to her.

"Kelly, your title in the agency is 'assistant' because that was the position you held when you worked with Dan Mathews. As his assistant, you took on a lot of responsibility and probably didn't get as much credit as you deserved."

"What's this all about, Joe? Dan was wonderful to work with, and he always made me feel appreciated."

"Maybe I'm phrasing it wrong," Joe said. "Let me try again. Kelly, I don't want you to think of yourself as my assistant, even though that's your position and a highly respected one at that. But on this case especially, I want you to think of yourself as my equal because that's how I feel about you."

"Just to set the record straight," Kelly teased, "I have always felt equal to you."

Joe laughed. "I give up! Let's go see Luke."

After introductions and a quick briefing on the case, Luke took Kelly and Joe into another room to view the security footage. Officer Mackey walked in just as they were finishing up. "Sorry to interrupt, but I felt you might want to see this." He handed the detective a folder. "We've narrowed it down to 125 registered white Ford vans between 2010 and 2014. Thompson thinks it's a 2010, and if so, then that would leave us with twenty-six in the Flagstaff area. I thought you'd want to start with those first." Luke glanced through the folder, then handed it back to Mackey.

"I want you and Hampson to contact each of the twenty-six and start eliminating. Any 2010 white vans that can't be located become a high priority." Before Mackey left, Detective Reynolds introduced him to Kelly and Joe. He told Mackey that it would be appropriate to share information with them should he not be available.

"I can appreciate your situation, Luke," Joe said. "You might not have much, but without that video, you'd have nothing to go on at this point. I know it's important to interview everyone in her life, but if the kidnapper's a complete stranger, then that makes finding him even more difficult. Speaking of interviewing, how did your meeting with Kristy go?"

"It went fine, but not as productive as I would've liked. She did provide the names of the men in Sara's life—which were few—and they all had a legitimate alibi. Kristy also mentioned a couple of hangouts she and Sara occasionally went to on weekends. Officer Beth Clark is checking on those, as well as the martial arts studio where Sara was a participant. This whole thing is very strange. No one saw anything at the strip mall, and they didn't know of anyone Sara might have had a problem with. Unless we find out who that white van belongs to, we're at a dead end."

"Did Kim answer his latest text?" Joe asked.

"Yes. I called her right after we talked and told her what to say. I haven't heard from her this morning yet."

Kelly was absorbing all the information and had remained quiet up to this point, but she also had questions. "Detective, did her neighbors notice any strange activity within the last few weeks of Sara's disappearance?"

"Unfortunately, no. I'd say there are a dozen units in the complex. Half of the residents are seniors, the rest are mostly working single women like Sara. There were only two units with young families. It doesn't seem like our suspect was anywhere near her apartment. And evidently he didn't go near her boutique until the morning he took her."

"He had to have known her from somewhere, and he was probably planning this for a while. Her abduction was too clean; he knew what he was doing."

"I agree, Kelly, and that's what makes it so difficult," said the detective.

"He also seemed to know her routine," said Joe. "He told her, according to what she documented, that he was watching her, and yet no one has seen a white van."

Kelly spoke up. "Here's another thought: What if he used a different vehicle when he was watching her and observing her routine other than the white van that he used when he kidnapped her?"

Luke looked over at Joe and smiled. "I see what you mean."

"Excuse me, Detective, but am I missing something here?" Kelly felt uncomfortable, and wondered if Luke was dismissing her input.

"I'm sorry, Kelly, and please call me Luke. Joe mentioned on the phone yesterday that you would be coming with him, and that he seldom worked a case without you. He said I would understand when I got to know you. Well, it didn't take me long to understand what Joe was talking about. Kelly, I'm glad to have you involved in the case, and I look forward to working with you."

Kelly didn't know whether to be annoyed with Joe or thankful that he spoke so highly of her. She chose the latter. "Thank you, Luke, for the vote of confidence." She avoided looking at Joe. "Would it be possible for Joe and me to see Sara's apartment after we go to the boutique?"

"Yes, definitely. I mentioned to Kim that you might want to do that, and she offered to meet you over there. I think it would be good for both of you to meet with her. She might even remember something that she hadn't thought of before."

They ended the meeting with Luke giving them the key to the boutique. They agreed to check in with each other later in the day, or sooner if either had relevant information.

Chapter Ten

After Sara apologized and explained why she got upset, Mister settled down. "Mister"—that's what he told Sara she could call him. He said he wanted to believe that she was sorry and he'd give her one more chance. He finally took the tape off her wrists and let her use the bathroom. He was comfortable she wouldn't try anything. There was nothing in the basement she could use to hit him with, and there were no windows for her to escape through. He went upstairs to get them something to eat, but he made sure to lock the door after he left.

Sara sat on the edge of the mattress, replaying everything that had transpired since she arrived at her boutique that morning. After telling him, when he made his way into the boutique, that her mother was due at any moment, she later had to convince him that Kim wouldn't be concerned to find her daughter not there when she arrived. Sara told him that Kim was used to her impulsive ways and would assume something came up and she just forgot. Since he had her phone, Sara suggested they send a text to Kim saying she'd left with a friend for a spur-of-the-moment getaway to make sure her mother wouldn't think something was wrong. Sara knew Kim wouldn't believe it. She also knew that by the time Kim got the text, she'd already have the police involved. That gave her hope.

Her thoughts faded when she heard the key turn in the door. Mister came in and handed her a paper plate containing a sandwich and potato chips. He gave her a plastic cup and told her she could get water from the bathroom. She sat there speechless. "Thank you" didn't seem appropriate.

"I went to the store and stocked up before I came to get you. I wanted to make sure I wouldn't have to leave for a while." Sara was numb and confused; she just sat there, holding the plate. "You better eat. I make a good sandwich—it's ham and cheese." She looked down at the food, knowing she'd better try it or fear upsetting him, but she didn't think she could get it down. Just as she started to take a bite, he got a text.

"It's your mother again," he said. "She wants you to call her. I think she's getting suspicious. I don't think she believes you're with a friend," Mister's voice began to escalate. "I need more time. She's got to believe you're on vacation! I don't want her bothering me. I want her to stop!" Sara, concerned over his increasing agitation, wondered what he'd do next. She thought about her mother and knew how worried she must be, not knowing whether her daughter was alive or dead. "I've got to go. I've got to think about what I'm going to do." He looked at Sara. "Eat your food!" he said angrily. "I'll be back!" Sara watched him leave, slamming the door and locking it. She heard him stomp up the stairs.

The food looked okay, but she couldn't get it down— her stomach was too queasy. She managed a potato chip, and that's all she could handle. She had to do something with the food before he came back. If he saw she didn't eat it, then what would he do? Breaking the sandwich up in little pieces, she flushed it down the toilet, saving the potato chips for later. An hour went by and he hadn't returned. All of a sudden, she heard music coming from upstairs. She recognized it as the same music she heard playing in the background on a couple of his calls. *What was he thinking? What was he going to do next?* Her mind was full of questions. Another hour went by and then the music stopped. She waited and waited, but he didn't return. All night she laid on the bed, restless and anxious, listening for footsteps. She wondered what he might do to her, and it terrified her. Her mind wouldn't allow her to dwell on it: She had to think about all the ways she could defend herself. Sometime toward morning, she fell asleep. Late that morning, he returned, but he didn't have food with him.

"I know what we're going to do," he announced, and then said nothing. Sara waited as she watched him walk back and forth, stop, stare at his phone, and do it all over again. Finally, she couldn't be still any longer, she had to know.

"Mister," she began in a soft voice, "what are we going to do?"

He walked over to the chair and sat down. "I have a plan. You're going to call your mother."

"What!?" Sara yelled, not sure how she'd react hearing her mother's voice on the other end. Would she break down and cry, causing Mister to become angry? She was excited and scared, all at the same time. Would this be her only chance to let her mother know that she was being held captive by a madman? But she didn't know where she was, and if she said that, then he might kill her right then and there.

"You're going to sound happy," he said. "You have to make her believe that you're with a friend and having a good time. If you don't, you'll regret it. You got that?"

Sara was concerned that when she heard her mother's voice, she wouldn't be able to hold it together, but it might be her only opportunity to let her know that she was alive. Sara was sure Kim wouldn't believe the texts were coming from her. Her mother knew her too well. She also believed that Kim was playing along, hoping to keep her daughter safe. She had to continue the act so Mister would think Kim was buying her story. She *could* do this, she *would* do this, she *had* to do this, she told herself. It was an opportunity to let Kim and the police know she was still alive.

Chapter Eleven

Kelly was surprised when she walked through the boutique at how normal everything looked. There was no sign of a struggle, nothing out of place, not even a speck of rubbish on the floor. It looked the way Sara might have left it—neat, orderly, and ready for the next day. She felt that whoever took Sara gave her little chance to react. She was anxious to meet Kim at the apartment and optimistic she'd find something the detective might've overlooked. Like Joe always said, it helps to have another pair of eyes when looking for clues.

When Kelly and Joe pulled into the apartment complex, they noticed a woman in front of the end unit on the second floor. They were sure it had to be Kim. As they got out of the car, the woman started down the stairs.

"Are you Kelly and Joe?" Kim asked.

"We are," said Joe.

"I thought I'd wait outside and watch for you in case you went to the wrong apartment. I'm Kim, Sara's mother. Detective Reynolds told me a little about you both. I'm very glad you're here to help."

"It's nice to meet you, Kim. I'm sorry it couldn't be under better circumstances," said Kelly. Joe echoed the sentiment.

They went into the apartment and Kim showed them around, as she did with the detective. Nothing stood out or caught their eye.

"Kim, did you get a call from Sara yet?" Joe asked, hoping she might've after he and Kelly left Luke.

"Not yet, but since I didn't get another text, Detective Reynolds thinks I might get a call today. I guess he told you they're monitoring my phone."

"Yes, he did," said Joe, hoping she'd get the call, but concerned what it might mean if she didn't.

"I'm so nervous. I hope I don't fall apart."

"You won't, Kim. You know how important it is to convince him that you believe Sara is with a friend having a good time. He no doubt will have you on speaker, so you can't say or ask anything you wouldn't want him to hear. You mentioned in one of your texts to Sara that you had important news to share with her. Have you thought about what you'll tell her should she ask?"

"If he read the text to her, she'll know I was just saying that so she won't ask unless he has her ask."

While Joe was talking to Kim, Kelly noticed a built-in bookcase in the corner of the room and went over to check it out. The first three shelves contained books, mostly fiction and memoirs, and the bottom shelf held two photo albums.

"Kim, excuse me, but have you seen these photo albums? Do you know what's in them?" Kelly asked.

"One contains pictures of Sara, starting from when she was a child and going through her college years. I think she started the other one a few years ago around the time she opened the boutique. I only glanced through it once, but mostly it contains pictures of her with friends having fun at cookouts, dinners, and a few camping trips."

Kelly took the second album over to the sofa and began going through it. Kim was right—lots of fun pictures with friends. Then she came to a page with three pictures of Kim and Sara at a restaurant. On the table was a cupcake with a candle in it. Standing behind them was a man with a hand on Kim's shoulder and the other hand on Sara's. "It looks like you're celebrating a birthday," Kelly said.

Kim leaned over to look at the picture. "Yes, it was Sara's birthday, and she had our waitress take a picture for us. I didn't realize she'd printed it out and put it in the album."

"Who's the man standing behind you?"

"He's one of the waiters, but he wasn't waiting on us that night. Sara and I always went to dinner twice a month. Most of the time, we went to this restaurant because it was one of Sara's favorite places to eat. They had a lot of farm-to-table items, and she tried to eat healthy when she could."

"If he wasn't waiting on you that night, then why is he in the picture?" Kelly asked.

"I'm not sure. He was always friendly and liked talking to Sara. Sara was easy to talk to. If we had a different waiter or waitress, he'd still come over just to say hello, if nothing else.

Joe looked at the picture. "It seems odd since he wasn't waiting on you that he'd impose himself in your picture."

"Sara was having a good time and everyone was very friendly. We didn't even realize he was in the picture until later. I guess we just thought he'd gotten caught up in wishing her a happy birthday. We didn't see him the last few times we went, so I don't know if he still works there."

There was something about that picture that piqued Kelly's interest. "Kim, do you know his name?"

"No, he didn't wear a name tag and we didn't think to ask. He may have mentioned it to Sara, but I don't remember."

"What is the name of the restaurant?"

"The Happy Camper."

"Would you mind if I borrow this picture? I'll return it in a few days." Before Kim could answer, her phone rang. Kelly noticed her hand shaking when she looked at the number.

"It's the same number his last text came from. It has to be Sara."

"You've got this, Kim. Take a deep breath, answer the phone, and put it on speaker," said Joe.

Chapter Twelve

Mister put a blindfold around Sara's eyes and taped her wrists together. Then he helped her upstairs and out to the van.

"Where are we going? I thought you wanted me to call my mother?"

"I do, and that's the plan, but you're not calling her from here. I thought you'd feel more relaxed if I took you to my secret secluded picnic area. I made breakfast sandwiches and brought a blanket to put on the ground. After you call your mother, we'll sit on the blanket and eat."

Sara couldn't believe what she was hearing. He sounded so normal, as if he was courting her and this was their first date. *Doesn't he realize how frightened I am of him, wondering every moment what's going to happen next? How long is this nice act going to last? When's he going to flip the switch and become angry? What does he want from me?*

They drove for about thirty minutes. When they got closer to their destination, Sara could tell by the feel of the road that it was no longer paved. When the van stopped, their journey wasn't over. They walked close to a mile through a wooded area before reaching the spot where he wanted to be—hidden from where the public usually goes. He told

Sara to stand still while he laid the blanket down and set the food on top of it, then he turned her around several times so she wouldn't know which direction they came from and removed the blindfold and tape from her wrists. She looked around and saw mostly trees. She tried desperately to look through them, but she still couldn't see where a road might be. She knew she couldn't run—he was faster—and where would she go? She had no idea where she was.

"It's beautiful out here, isn't it, Sara?" The blanket was placed in a small clear area in front of a tiny creek.

"Yes, it is," she said, relieved to be outside for a while.

"Sit down on the blanket and we'll call your mother. We'll put her on speaker so I can hear. If all goes well, then we'll eat." He dialed the number, put the phone on speaker, and handed it to Sara.

"Hello?"

"Hi, Mom, it's Sara."

"Sara, I was hoping you'd call today. How are you doing? Are you having a good time?"

"Yes. I'm sorry I didn't call you and tell you about my plans before, but it all happened so quickly, and we've been on the go ever since."

"What are you doing today?" Kim asked.

"Actually, we're having a quiet morning before our busy afternoon. We're enjoying an early picnic, and it's very pretty here. Lots of beautiful trees, and we're sitting in front of a picturesque little creek." Mister grabbed the phone and shook his head at her. He covered the speaker and whispered to her not to say another word about what the area looked like. She nodded and he handed the phone back.

"It sounds like a nice place to have a picnic." Kim responded calmly. "We used to do a lot of road trips and picnics along the way when you were a child. Does it look like any place we might've been before?"

"No, Mom, I've never been here before." Mister gave her a sign to wrap it up. He told her before she called to make it clear that she wouldn't be in touch while she was gone. "I've got to go, Mom. My friend, Alice, is packing up, and she needs my help carrying stuff to the van." Mister gave her an angry look. "Alice keeps reminded me that it's an SUV, not a van, but I guess they all look the same to me."

"Before you hang up, can you at least tell me where you are?"

"I'll fill you in on everywhere we've been when I get home. Don't expect to hear from me until I return. I'll be busy and on the go. I love you, Mom." Sara started to choke up, and before she could tell Kim goodbye, Mister ended the call.

Chapter Thirteen

He sat there quietly for several minutes staring at the creek before he spoke. He turned and looked at Sara. "Why did you tell your mother what this place looks like?"

Sara didn't want him to dwell any longer on what she said and responded immediately. "She thinks I'm in another state, she has no idea I'm still in Arizona. You heard her—she believes I'm okay and with my friend. It's so beautiful here, I just got caught up in the moment."

"Okay," he said. "I guess she didn't sound worried, so maybe she does believe you're out of town with a friend." He opened the bag of food, pulled out two breakfast sandwiches, two bananas, a large bottled water, and two plastic cups. "The sandwich is ham, egg, and cheese," he said, handing Sara her share. "I hope you like it. It's one of my favorite breakfast foods."

"Thank you," Sara said, trying to sound normal. She was hungry, but she didn't know if she could eat. She kept thinking about her conversation with Kim. She knew her mother was aware that she'd been taken against her will and never would've left without telling her. Sara thought the police must be involved and advising Kim how to respond to texts and calls, otherwise her mother would've been frantic. She never could've been that calm on the phone without being coached. Sara could only imagine how scared and worried her mother must be, but at least for now, she knew she was alive.

Mister didn't talk much while they ate. Sara studied everything around her, hoping something would feel familiar. She did her share of hiking, but she'd never been to this area. She also had a good opportunity to study Mister. He still wore the cap pulled down to his eyes, but she was convinced she knew him from somewhere, but where?

When they were through eating and ready to leave, Mister put the blindfold back on Sara and taped her wrists again.

"Why do you have to do this?" she asked. "I'm not going to run—I wouldn't know where to go, and besides, you're much faster than I am." Being able to run a marathon didn't mean you were fast, but Sara did have the stamina to run long distances should the opportunity present itself.

"I don't trust you yet," said Mister. "I don't want you to know where we're going or where you're staying. I know we're meant to be together, but you don't know that yet. I had to take you like I did because you wouldn't have left your business and come on your own."

Sara couldn't grasp his logic. *How can he think taking me against my will is going to win me over? And why me? He must know me from somewhere, but why can't I place him? Is he one of the bank tellers I go to? I know I've seen him before.* Sara always seemed to have a difficult time associating people she met when she saw them outside of their work environment. One time, when Sara was at the grocery store, she ran into the receptionist from her dental office. She thought she looked familiar, but she couldn't place where she'd seen her. Sara was embarrassed when the receptionist recognized her immediately.

Maybe I can get Mister to tell me more about himself. "Mister, if you wanted to be with me, why didn't you just ask me out like most men would've done?"

"You don't like to date, and it would've really upset me if you said no. I've had a lot of bad things happen to me lately, and I'm not in the mood to take anymore rejection. I'm trying to be nice to you and give you time to get to know me, because if you reject me, it won't be pretty. Now let's get out of here."

Sara thought it interesting that he said she didn't like to date, and wondered how he came up with that. They were almost to the van when she heard children laughing. "Mister, I hear children. Won't they wonder why I look like this? Why my eyes are covered and my hands bound? They might run and tell someone, then what would happen?" she asked, wanting to give the impression that she was concerned about him. She was also hoping to get some insight as to where they might be.

"They can't see us," he said. "They're on the other side of the trees and away from here. They can't see us."

Sara decided to keep up the act—maybe she could prolong the inevitable. "Thank you for the picnic brunch, it was very nice. Mister, the main reason I don't like to date is because most men want to rush things. I don't like that. I like to take things slow, get to know someone over a period of time and make sure I'm sharing my feelings with the right person. That's what makes a relationship special. You seem to understand that, and I want you to know I appreciate it." Sara hoped this would give her more time to figure out how she was going to get away from him.

He didn't say a word, but when they got to the van, he gently helped her into her seat.

Chapter Fourteen

Kim did well on the call with Sara. She said the right things, giving Sara a chance to provide clues—a wooded area with a creek. Is this where he was hiding her, or were they on the move and that was just a stopping place? At least for now they knew she was alive, but for how long? These types of situations could change quickly, but they reassured Kim that the phone call was a positive sign.

Shortly after Sara's call, Joe heard from Luke. He said they'd picked up a ping in an area with a small open space and a forest behind it. He was headed that way and asked Joe if he and Kelly wanted to join him. Joe said yes, he'd go, but Kelly chose to go to the restaurant instead. She was eager to find out whatever she could on the waiter. There was something about the picture in Sara's photo album that intrigued her, and she felt it might be important.

Arriving at the restaurant a few minutes before the lunch crowd gave Kelly an opportunity to talk with two of the waitresses. Kelly showed them the picture, and they confirmed that he did work there for a while but left a few weeks ago under questionable circumstances. One of the waitresses, Jessie, said his name was Ross Chatfield, and he only worked part-time because he had a full-time job elsewhere.

Kelly asked if either of them remembered seeing Sara and Kim there. Jessie spoke up.

"I waited on them a few times which irritated Ross. We don't have assigned tables like most restaurants, but we do have designated areas where two or three of us work at a time. Most of the time I, along with Ross and Linda, worked the back section. Sara and her mom usually sat in there by the window. I liked waiting on them. They never complained and tipped good.

The night of Sara's birthday, Ross was in the kitchen picking up an order, so I got to their table first. When he saw me handing them menus, he came over and told me that he'd take care of them and I could go wait on another table. I forced a smile and said thank you, but since he was busy with four other tables and I only had two at the time, I'd continue with them. Then I genuinely smiled at Sara and her mom and said I'd be back with water and take their order. As Ross walked away, he gave me a look that made me very uncomfortable."

"Do either of you know why he left here, or where his other job is?" They both shook their head no. The other waitress left to greet arriving customers, but Jessie lingered.

"Jessie, is anyone else available who might be able to provide additional information about Ross Chatfield?" asked Kelly.

"Are you a cop, or a friend looking for him?"

"Neither, I work for a private investigative agency. We think talking with Ross might shed some light on a situation we're investigating, but I'm having trouble locating him." Kelly didn't want to alarm the waitress by giving her more information than she needed to hear.

"I'm sorry I'm not more help, but I didn't pay much attention to the guy. He just rubbed me the wrong way, and other then work, our paths never crossed. You should talk to our manager, Sophie. She's the one who hired him. He must have passed her rigid questioning and background check or he wouldn't have been working here. She's pretty particular and tries to avoid people who she feels might become a problem."

"Is Sophie here," asked Kelly.

"Not yet, but she should be here in about thirty minutes. If you'd like to wait, I'll be glad to get you a glass of water or a cup of coffee."

"Thank you, Jessie. I'd like to wait, and I'd like to see a menu. I might as well eat while I'm waiting, and if it's okay with you, I'd like to sit in your section." Jessie smiled and took Kelly to a table by the window.

Luke and Joe searched the area where the suspect's phone pinged, but after more than an hour, they still didn't find any remnants of a picnic or any sign of Sara having been there. They walked through pinyon and pine trees until they came across a small creek. The trees thinned giving way to grass, weeds, and a few wildflowers growing along the creek's bank. A couple of areas supported room for a picnic, but nothing appeared disturbed.

"It would've been nice to find them hiding in a tent, but I guess that would've been too easy," said Luke. "I don't know, Joe, maybe they weren't even here. It's possible he just stopped long enough to have Sara make the call."

"They were here," said Joe. "Sara wouldn't have mentioned a creek and trees unless she was here. She was trying to give us a clue."

"That might be, but what if he had her say those things just to throw us off. According to the ping, they were somewhere in the area, but for how long? If they were here having a picnic like Sara said, then we probably missed them by minutes, and that's damn frustrating," he sighed. "Come on, Joe, we're done here."

Kelly was still picking at her salad when someone sat down in the chair across from her. "Hi, I'm Sophie. Jessie said you wanted to talk to me about Ross Chatfield."

Chapter Fifteen

Kelly's head was spinning from all the information Jessie and Sophie had provided about Ross Chatfield, and she was anxious to get back to the precinct and share it with Luke and Joe. When she called Joe to tell him she was on her way, he told her about the disappointing and unproductive excursion he and Luke had through the woods.

"Joe, I'm ninety-nine percent sure who the kidnapper is," Kelly said excitedly.

"Are you kidding me? How did you come up with that?"

"Too much detail to give over the phone. I'll be there shortly, but to save time, have Luke get an address on a Ross Chatfield and check with Mackey to see if Ross is one of the registered owners of a white van."

When Kelly entered the detective's office, Luke immediately handed her a sheet of paper. "That's the information on Ross Chatfield." He owns a 2010 white Ford Econoline, he's married to Betty, and as you can see by the address, they live across town. I'm sure he wouldn't have taken Sara there."

"No, he wouldn't have," said Kelly. "He and his wife have been separated for months."

"How do you know this?" asked Joe. "Is he the guy in the picture taken at the restaurant with Kim and Sara?"

"Yes." Kelly told them about the conversation with Jessie. "Jessie was helpful, but I got a lot more information from the manager, Sophie, about who Ross Chatfield used to be and how he changed in the last several months."

"Did Sophie happen to know where he's living now?" asked Luke.

"No. Sophie said he never picked up his last check and didn't give a forwarding address."

"So there's no way of knowing where he might've taken Sara," said Joe. "Kelly, what else did Sophie tell you?"

Kelly told them about the background check Sophia did on Ross, and that he came up clean. "There were no records of any prior arrest, warrants, or even traffic violations. She said he was pleasant and easy to get along with until the last six months of his employment. That's when things started to change."

"How so?" asked Luke.

"Ross's wife, Betty, is an accountant for an upscale law office. She saw the type of clients and money that came through the firm. Ross had a full-time job as a mechanic, but never made enough money to satisfy Betty. He started working part-time at the restaurant because they paid well and the tips were good, but it wasn't good enough for Betty. She became more and more frustrated, and resentful, that she couldn't live comfortably the way the lawyers she worked for did.

Ross confided in Mike, another waiter at The Happy Camper, about his declining marriage. It seems Ross couldn't do anything right in Betty's eyes, and she started making him feel like a loser. He still loved Betty, but she was falling out of love with him. The final straw came when the auto shop let Ross go after the owner's son moved back to town and needed a job. Ross couldn't find another job, and Betty had had enough and kicked him out. It was then when Ross's personality began to change. He wanted to work more hours at the restaurant, but Sophie couldn't give him more hours without taking them away from someone else. He became aggressive and tried to secure all the tables he could in his section."

Joe shook his head. "Since losing Betty and his job at the auto shop, it sounds like he was becoming more desperate as his money dwindled."

"Mike told Sophie that Ross wanted to move in with him. After watching his behavior become more erratic, Mike didn't want him around him and his wife, besides, they were moving in a few weeks back to their home town in Iowa, so he told Ross that moving in with him was not an option. Ross got very upset, yelling at Mike repeating, 'I thought you were my friend!' Then he started calling Mike on a daily basis, wanting his help in finding a job so Betty would take him back. It got so bad that by the time Mike left town, he changed his phone number. After their last conversation, which concerned Mike, he went to Sophie and told her everything—that Ross kept rambling about not needing Betty anymore and how he'd show her. He was going to find someone who would care more about him than money. He'd treat her good unless she made him feel like a loser the way Betty did."

"Is that when Sophie fired him?" asked Luke.

"No, that came a few weeks later. Sophie said she needed a concrete reason to fire him other than hearsay. She knew his behavior was becoming stranger and stranger, especially with some of the waitresses, but overall, he worked hard and treated the customers well. Then one night, Sophie observed him taking tips off tables that weren't his. She had cameras in the dining area, but most of the staff didn't know they were there. The next day, she called Ross into her office and confronted him. He denied it until she showed him the evidence. He tried giving her all kinds of excuses, but she was having none of it and told him the cameras don't lie. She said he could pick up his last check on Friday, but after that, he was never to return or she'd call the police."

Joe wanted to know why Sophie felt she had to pay Ross if he was taking money that belonged to someone else.

"She was trying to keep him calm, and she thought if she paid him, he wouldn't retaliate. But he went berserk and said she was no better than Betty, and one day she'd regret firing him. Then he kicked the chair and stormed out. She never saw him again."

"I wonder what made him decide on Sara?"

Kelly weighed Joe's question before answering. "Well, she was a customer at the restaurant, and she was always nice to him. But according to Kim, she was that way with everyone. Maybe he read more into it because Sara usually came in with her mother and not another man. Some of that could've played into his decision."

They talked a while longer, then Luke got up and grabbed his keys. "Come on, let's go. It's time to pay Betty a visit."

Chapter Sixteen

They arrived at Betty Chatfield's just as she was pulling into the driveway. Luke drove past the house and went around the block a few times. He wanted Betty inside and settled before approaching her. He assumed that she was returning from work, and he didn't want a question-and-answer session outside. The veteran detective understood the importance of a comfortable environment, especially for what might turn out to be a difficult interview.

There was nothing unusual about the well-kept modest home. It was pretty much what Luke, Joe, and Kelly expected to find—small eat-in kitchen, quaint living room, and probably a couple of bedrooms. But they weren't prepared for how Betty was going to look. She was tall and slender with very short chestnut-colored hair combed in a pixie style. She could have passed for Sara's sister, the similarities were so uncanny. Confused by their presence, Betty was reluctant to talk about Ross.

"We're separated, soon to be divorced, and I don't have anything to say about him."

Detective Reynolds cut to the chase. "We're investigating a kidnapping and we need your cooperation. A young woman's life is in danger. We have evidence to support that Ross is the person who took her."

Betty slumped back in her chair in disbelief. "What do you want from me?" she asked, still trying to process that Ross was capable of kidnapping.

"Information," said the detective. "When was the last time you saw Ross?"

"I've only seen him once since I told him to leave, and that's been several months ago. I quit answering his calls after I told him I'd talk when the divorce papers were ready."

"Did you know he lost his job at the restaurant?"

"No. I knew he worked there, so I avoided the place."

"The restaurant doesn't have a forwarding address for him. Do you know where he's living now?"

"No, and I don't care to know. I don't know what I can say to help you. I'm not responsible for what he does."

Detective Reynolds paused. It was time to shift the questioning. Betty was becoming annoyed, and he decided a feminine touch might be helpful. The three of them were seated on the sofa, Kelly in the middle. Betty sat in the recliner to their left. He turned to Kelly and nodded. She understood and took over.

"Betty, I can appreciate your frustration. You thought he was out of your life, and this is bringing up a lot of feelings that you don't care to revisit. I hope you'll indulge us a little longer and understand our only purpose in being here is to gain insight in how we can locate Ross and bring this young woman safely home to her family."

Betty sighed. "I'm sorry, but I can't think of any helpful information that I'd be able to provide."

"Sometimes we don't realize we might know more than we think we do," said Kelly. "I'd like to ask a few more questions, and maybe something will come to you. This might not seem relevant, but please bear with me. Betty, during your marriage, did you and Ross have a favorite getaway place?"

"Not really. We didn't have a lot of extra cash to take nice vacations"

"Did you ever go fishing or camping?"

"Not me, that's not my style."

"What about Ross?"

Betty thought for a moment. "His grandparents had an old run-down house out in the boonies. They left the place to Ross's parents, but they moved out of state a couple of years ago and haven't really done anything with it. Ross has a key and he liked to hang out there. He'd keep his hunting rifle loaded, hoping a deer or wild boar would wander by." She stopped and looked at all three of them. "Now that I think about it, that might be where he's been living. His parents keep the electricity on because they know Ross likes to go there. They were counting on him to do some of the repairs in hopes of selling it one day."

Joe jumped in with the next question. "Have you ever been there?"

"Only once, but that was enough for me,"

Joe couldn't resist. "Let me guess—not your style."

"That's right, and get this: Ross thought it would be fun to live in that run-down place while he fixed it up. I said, no thanks! It was too far from anything, including my work, and I certainly didn't want anyone to think I was a country hick."

"Heaven forbid," said Joe. Kelly discreetly nudged him with her foot and once again took over.

"Betty, can you tell us how to get to this place?"

"I wouldn't have a clue. Like I said, I've only been there once, and that was years ago."

"What about his parents? Can you give us their names and a phone number?"

"I don't have that information. They didn't like me. They thought I was too uppity, just because I like nice things. I thought they were snooty. I never called them, so their contact info was meaningless to me. You know how it is—sometimes you just can't get along with in-laws."

"One more question, Betty," she looked at Luke and Joe, "unless Joe or Detective Reynolds has a question, but do you have a picture of the house?"

Betty gave Kelly a look like she thought she must be out of her mind. "Seriously? I told you how I felt about that eyesore. Why would I have a picture of it?"

Kelly considered her question. "I wondered if the family or Ross might have taken pictures over the years, especially when his grandparents were living there. Is there any chance there could be a picture of the old homestead in a photo album?"

Without saying a word, Betty got up and went to a back bedroom. She came back with a box and set it down on the small glass coffee table in front of the trio. "That's the last of Ross's stuff. He must've forgotten it was here because he never came back for it. There might be some old pictures, but mostly it's high school yearbooks, a pocket knife, and some other odds and ends."

"We've taken up enough of your time," said Detective Reynolds. "Why don't we take the box with us and bring it back when we're through with it?"

"That's fine with me," said Betty. "As far as I'm concerned, you can keep it, and then he won't have an excuse to come back here."

They thanked Betty for her time and help, but as they were leaving, Kelly thought of one more thing.

"Betty, do you have any idea, now that Ross has lost his jobs, how he's supporting himself?"

"Oh, sure! Mommy and Daddy. When Ross lost his mechanic job, his parents sent him a check each month to help out until he could find another full-time job. They sent it to a post office box he'd set up when he moved out." She paused, "I didn't even think of the P.O. box. There've been times when I had to send some paperwork to him, so I have the address if you want it, but I don't know what good it will do you."

"That would be greatly appreciated. Thank you, Betty. You've been very helpful."

Chapter Seventeen

The post office was closed when they left Betty's, so they went back to the precinct to go through the contents of the box she gave them. It did contain some of Ross Chatfield's personal items, but unfortunately there were no photos of old run-down homes. However, the visit with Betty was productive and gave Detective Reynolds and his team a new direction to pursue. Finding Ross Chatfield's grandparent's home would be challenging, but they were encouraged to have a clue where Ross might be hiding Sara. There wasn't much more they could do that evening except plan for the next day. Over delivered pizza and soft drinks, they discussed what needed to be done. Joe and Kelly would contact the realtors and research court records of older homes in rural areas while Luke and Tom Mackey viewed camera footage from the post office. After the day's events, and feeling more encouraged, morning couldn't come soon enough. They were anxious to find Sara.

Luke Reynolds had one more stop before heading home. A phone call seemed inadequate with all Kim had been through. He wanted to tell her in person.

"Detective Reynolds, is everything okay? Did you find Sara?" Kim asked with fear and hope in her voice, surprised to see the detective on her doorstep at eight.

"No, Kim, we didn't find Sara, but we have a better idea where she is and who took her." Luke, still standing in the doorway, wondered if Kim might have someone inside since she didn't invite him in. "I wanted to come by and tell you in person. I know it's late, but would you mind if I come in?"

"I'm sorry, Detective, yes, please come in. Excuse my manners, but I'm surprised to see you here. It must be pretty important for you to come to my house instead of calling." She held the door open and the detective walked in.

Luke liked the feel of Kim's home—it was warm and inviting. Same open concept as Sara's, but larger and less modern, more of a southwestern flair. The turquoise and coral throws and pillows nicely accentuated the light tan sofa and loveseat. The wall behind the sofa was adorned with dreamcatchers and colorful woven baskets.

"Please have a seat," Kim said. "You look tired, Detective. I'm anxious to hear what you have to say, but can I fix you a cup of coffee first?"

The detective *was* tired: It had been a long day. He was sure he looked a mess. He took his hand and rubbed down his windblown, slightly greying hair and wondered if he had anything in his mustache or the closely groomed beard he liked to sport. Luke never understood why, but he felt more masculine with facial hair. He thought it softened his blue eyes and long eyelashes, minimizing the uncomfortable compliments he hated responding to.

"Thank you, Kim. If it's not too much trouble, I would like a cup of coffee. Black please." As he watched Kim in the kitchen making the coffee, he understood where Sara got her looks. Kim's hair was a little longer and softly curled, but there was no mistaking they were mother and daughter. Kim's extra few pounds suited her well. Luke guessed her age between forty-eight and fifty-two. She was still very attractive, and he wondered why she'd never remarried.

"Here, Detective," Kim said, setting the coffee mug on the end table close to him.

"Thank you, Kim, and you can call me Luke." Kim smiled, but he could tell how anxious she was. He wasted no time bringing her up to date on Kelly's visit with Jessie and Sophie, but he was careful not to give too much detail on Ross's erratic behavior. He didn't want to worry her any more than she already was.

Kim was shocked to learn that it was the waiter from Sara's favorite restaurant. He'd always been so nice to them. "Why Sara?" she asked.

"We wondered that also until we met his soon-to-be ex-wife." He told Kim how much Sara resembled Betty. "After losing his jobs and his wife, he clearly wasn't thinking straight." Luke wanted to tell Kim as much as he felt he could, but he also wanted to be careful how he said it. "He may have thought by taking Sara and having her all to himself, he could persuade her to fall in love with him." Kim looked horrified. Luke continued.

"There's a good possibility he's holding Sara at his grandparents' old house. We just have to find it, and Kelly and Joe will be working on that. Officer Mackey and I will go to the post office and try to get a pattern of when he stops in. I'll have an officer posted in the area and if someone in a white van shows up, he's to discreetly follow him and contact us."

"That's very encouraging, Detective . . ."

"Luke, please," the detective said.

"Okay . . . Luke . . . but the thought of Sara having to spend another night there terrifies me."

"I'm sure it does. I know it's difficult, but we know she's alive—he took her on a picnic and he let her call you. I don't think he wants to hurt her." He wasn't sure that was true, but he knew it was what she needed to hear. "Kim, tell me more about Sara. I know she's a kind person and everyone likes her, but what are some of her other traits?" Luke wanted to get a sense of Sara's coping skills, how she did under pressure and how well she handled stressful situations.

"Sara's a very confident person. She does well when dealing with a challenge. She's the peacemaker in the family." Kim smiled as she thought about the many times Sara was asked to intervene. "She's helped resolve differences between her cousins as well as her friends. Even as a teenager, whenever anyone had a problem, they were drawn to her. She always seemed to know the right thing to say, like the time she helped her twin cousins. The twins, Janet and Joan are fraternal and as different as night and day. Janet was the extrovert and wanted to be in the midst of all the action; Joan was shy and felt awkward in large groups. As they got older, Janet wanted to be involved in every social activity, and she always wanted Joan to go with her, but Joan didn't want to go. She preferred staying at home reading a book, watching T.V., or chatting with a friend on the phone. Janet was hurt and thought Joan just didn't want to be with her anymore. Sara helped Janet understand that it wasn't Joan she didn't want to be with; it was being in a large group that made her uncomfortable. Sara suggested that Janet invite Joan along to a movie or lunch with a friend or two, but respect her discomfort when attending large gatherings with people she didn't know. With Sara's help, Janet and Joan learned to appreciate and respect each other's differences, and to this day they remain close."

Luke watched Kim beam when she spoke of Sara. He wished he had a child. His twenty-year marriage to Ruth had been good, but she never wanted children. Ruth liked being on the go and didn't want to be tied down with kids. Then five years ago she told Luke she was tired of his unpredictable hours, and the marriage ended. He didn't blame her. He understood they were on different paths and the divorce was amicable. They each went their separate ways, but he missed not having children. At fifty-three, the thoughts of having kids were behind him.

"Kim, Sara will know what to do, and we're going to find her before anything happens." Luke knew at that point that this case had become personal. He could only imagine how he'd feel if it was his daughter who'd been kidnapped. Even though he had nieces he loved, he sure wouldn't want anything happening to them.

"I want to believe that," said Kim. "I *have* to believe it or I'll go out of my mind. Thank you for stopping by, it means a lot. I feel more hopeful now than I have since this nightmare began."

Chapter Eighteen

After they returned from the picnic brunch Mister had surprised her with, he removed the blindfold and once again took the tape off Sara's wrists.

"I've been thinking about what you said," he began. "Sara, you said you didn't like to date because most men want to rush things, and you don't like that. You said I was different. I want to believe that you meant what you said. I want you to like me, Sara, but if I find out you were just playing me . . . I promise you, things will get ugly. I told you before, I can't take anymore rejection. I've lost everything already, so if this doesn't work out, I don't care what happens. Do you understand?" Sara stared at him a moment and then nodded. She didn't want to say anything, too afraid she'd say something wrong. Sitting on the edge of the bed, looking up at him, he seemed much larger as he towered over her.

"I want to do something special for you tomorrow. I'll leave you alone now while I go upstairs and figure it all out." Without saying another word, he left the room and she waited for the click of the key in the lock.

Sara felt numb and continued sitting on the bed, trying not to think about his next move. Then she got up and walked around, taking notice of the cinder block walls and cold concrete floor. Even the spiderwebs in the corners of the room had no life left in them. She went over to the door—her only means of escape from that dreadful windowless room—and peered in the keyhole, knowing full well there was no way she could open it from inside. Frustrated, she paced back and forth then she finally sat in the wooden chair that was still secured to the floor. Time was running out and she knew it. The silence was deafening, but it was soon broken by the sound of music—the same music she'd been hearing, but this time she paid more attention to it. There was something familiar about that instrumental tune, other than when he played it.

"Where have I heard that song?" she said out loud. Then it came to her. She sprung from the chair. 'Ebb Tide'! The Happy Camper!" Sara had only heard it there on a couple of occasions, but she remembered the waiter saying that he and his wife used to dance to it. "The waiter, yes, the waiter!" She had a lightbulb moment when she finally realized who Mister was. "I can see the resemblance now, even with his cap." She continued talking out loud as if hearing her own voice was comforting. "I know he told me his name, but what was it? Come on, Sara, think." She began going through the alphabet of all the names she knew until it finally came to her. "Ross, that's it! He's Ross, the waiter from the restaurant."

Sara sat back down on the chair, struggling to make sense of this new revelation. Thinking back to the few occasions when he waited on them, she remembered him as being friendly and sociable. But most of the time when he was at their table, she was either looking at the menu, eating her food, or having a conversation with her mom. She paid no more attention to him then she would've Jessie or any other server.

What now? What do I do? Do I tell him I know who he is, or do I wait and see what he has planned for tomorrow? Her mind was buzzing. *I know the right decision could change everything. Should I tell him or not? His behavior's unpredictable, and I'm not sure which way to go. If he finds out that I know who he is, will he get upset? Or since he was a friendly and conscientious waiter, will he think the chances of me falling in love with him will be greater? Could I use that to my advantage?* Sara had a lot to think about, and she knew the answers to those questions might determine how the next day went. A sense of impending doom hung over her as she thought about tomorrow.

I have to figure this out. Sara continued to turn everything over in her mind. *I have to get into his psyche and find a way to catch him off guard. If I don't get away tomorrow, I doubt I'll have another chance,* she concluded. *I have to get away from here or die trying. I can't live like this!*

Chapter Nineteen

Kelly spent most of the morning on the phone, checking with realtors to see if anyone knew anything about the Chatfields or where a home like theirs might be. She wasn't having any luck, but she did learn where older homes with acreage could be found. When she felt she had enough information, she walked into Joe's office and announced her plans.

"I have a list of some possibilities, and I'm on my way to check them out."

"Excuse me," said Joe. "Are you referring to homes where Ross might be hiding Sara?"

"Yes, of course I am. What do you think I've been doing all morning?"

"Kelly, you can't go by yourself. This man is dangerous, and if confronted, there's no telling what he might do."

She looked at him and shook her head. "I know what to do, I'm not stupid. If I see a white van in front of an old house, I'll call Luke and have officers meet me there."

"I know you're capable of taking care of yourself, but so was Sara. I'm just concerned, and I'd like to go with you. I've had every available investigator in this office researching properties and court records, so I have a list too. I was getting ready to check with you to see if you wanted to go with me.

Maybe some of your properties are in the same area as mine. It makes sense for us to go together. We can compare our lists and combine those that are close together."

Kelly knew he was right, but she hated to admit it. "Once in a while, you make sense, and I guess it's better than taking two cars. You know what they say—two heads are better than one. But that remains to be seen," she said sarcastically, with a smile. She always reverted to sarcasm with Joe when she wanted to lighten the mood. Before they left, she asked Joe if he'd heard anything from Luke that morning.

"I just hung up with him when you walked in. I'll tell you about it in the car, no need wasting time here." He handed Kelly his list so she could compare it to hers. "When you're through, let me know where you want to start."

While driving along the route Kelly had chosen, Joe told her about his conversation with Luke and what he and Mackey found out at the post office. "The cameras showed Ross picking up his mail on Wednesdays and Saturdays. Luke said he didn't deviate; it was always on those days. He seems to be a creature of habit. Anyway, Luke said since today's Wednesday, he'll have an officer in an unmarked car staked out in the parking lot and another one waiting on the side street. If Ross shows up, the two officers will alternate following him until traffic thins and it becomes too obvious that he's being followed. Then they'll pull back and continue at a safe distance."

"Is Luke concerned if the officers pull Ross over and bring him in for questioning that he'll clam up and put Sara in a more desperate situation?" Kelly asked.

"Yes, and we'd lose valuable time. He's also concerned if the officers lose sight of him—and they might have to for a while to keep him from becoming suspicious—that Ross could have time to get Sara and escape from a different route before being seen."

"I can understand his concern," said Kelly.

"He also mentioned something that I think you'll find interesting."

"Oh, what's that?"

"He stopped by Kim's on his way home last night. He wanted to tell her in person that we now know who has Sara and where he might've taken her."

"I bet she was shocked to find out it was the waiter from Sara's favorite restaurant."

"I'm sure she was. Luke said he learned a lot about Sara during his conversation with Kim. He feels Sara has a strong psyche, and he said if anyone could survive this ordeal, it would be her." Kelly smiled and nodded her head, and Joe noticed. "What're you thinking?' he asked.

"It's nice to know someone else has come to the same conclusion that I've already reached."

Joe gave her a puzzled look. "And what other conclusions have you reached that you're keeping from me?" Kelly remained quiet. "Kelly, talk to me. Do you know what's going to happen to Sara?"

"Realistically, I have no way of knowing what's going to happen to her."

"But you know more than the rest of us. You're sensing something, so why won't you tell me? I know you, Kelly, I know the feelings you get." Between Cripple Creek and working together in Sedona, Joe had learned a lot about Kelly's intuition.

She sighed. "I'm hoping I'm wrong, but if we don't find Sara soon, she may be in more danger from wild boars than she is from Ross Chatfield."

"What?"

"I know it sounds crazy, and please don't mention it to Luke."

"You have to give me more, Kelly. What're you seeing?"

"Nothing, and that's why I didn't want to mention it. I'm not getting anything else at the moment. I just see Sara running and I see wild boars, but I don't know what it means."

"Could it be that Sara is running from Ross and, for whatever reason, you see him as a boar?"

"No. Sara might be running from Ross, but it's three wild boars that keep coming to me. I hope it means something else. I don't always see things clearly at first. I'm not a psychic, but I've come to accept that I'm intuitive. Sometimes I have a strong sense of things, but I don't always know what it means or when it's going to happen. I can't will it."

Kelly was interrupted by the GPS announcing they had arrived at their designated address. One look and it was obvious Sara couldn't have been at that location. The house looked well-kept, and there was a swing set and trampoline in the yard.

Kelly entered the next address. "We can't get discouraged, we've just started," she said. "I feel we're going to find the house, but I don't know if Sara will be there."

Chapter Twenty

Continuing their search, Kelly and Joe had decided that it made sense to begin at the farthest property out and work their way back to town. Kelly felt they'd have a better chance of finding Sara in a more remote area surrounded by lots of trees. She remembered Betty saying that Ross kept his hunting rifle loaded, hoping to see a deer or wild boar. Kelly pictured the house nestled in the woods.

Joe slowed down when they approached a side road with an older house off to the right. He turned and slowly drove past to see if anyone was living there. It didn't have a garage and lacked vehicles.

"What do you think, Kelly? I know it's not on our list, but it does look vacant."

"It's worth a look, but I don't see a white van, and look around—there are neighbors not too far away. I guess we're not necessarily looking for a white van. If Ross went to the post office, the van would be gone. Let's check it out. If someone comes to the door, we can always pretend to be realtors looking for property to sell."

Joe's list included properties belonging to anyone named Chatfield, but if Ross's grandparents were his mother's parents instead of his father's, then the property might not be deeded under Chatfield. Kelly had narrowed her list to older rural properties that might be vacant, up for sale, or had been for sale at one time. Either way, any property fitting the description needed to be considered.

They pulled into the driveway of the house off the side road. Before getting out of the car, they noticed a child at the front door letting a dog out. The dog took off toward the back of the house and the child, who looked to be around twelve, saw them and walked over to the car. Kelly lowered the window.

"Can I help you?" he asked.

"I think we're at the wrong house," Kelly replied. "We're looking for Mr. Chatfield's place. Would you know someone by that name?"

"No. I don't know too many people around here. We just moved in a few months ago."

"He drives an older white van. Have you seen a van like that?"

"Not that I remember. I don't pay much attention to cars and trucks. At least not yet," he said with a grin, showing a full set of braces. I'm sure I will in a couple of years. Do you want me to ask my mom?"

"No, but thank you. We have some other places to check out. I'm sure we'll find him." Kelly didn't want to waste anymore time. They had a long day ahead of them and many stops to make. She studied her list and punched in another address.

"Joe, this one's about twenty minutes from here. It's in a remote area on twenty-five acres and no one's living there—at least that's what the realtor indicated."

"Sounds good." Joe had something on his mind and he felt this would be a good time to discuss it. "Kelly, do you consider us friends?"

Kelly was surprised by the question. "That's a strange thing to ask, considering everything we've been through together; Cripple Creek, Sedona, and now working together full-time. I thought we were friends even before I became your employee." She could tell by the look on his face that she should have left the word "employee" off.

"I'd appreciate it if you'd quit referring to yourself as my employee. If I remember correctly, when I took over the agency from Dan, I wanted you to be a partner, but you refused."

"I know. I don't know why I said it like that, except I was surprised and confused by your question. Why would you ask that? Don't you consider us friends?" The windows were down and her shoulder-length auburn hair was blowing into her green Irish eyes.

"Of course I consider us friends," said Joe. "Kelly, I've been thinking about something," he paused, not quite sure if he should continue.

"And," she said, anxious to know what he had on his mind.

"Okay, I'll get to the point. Kelly, you've been staying in a motel in Flagstaff close to my house so you'd be available at a moment's notice and not have to drive from Sedona. You know I have a spare bedroom and extra bath—which I've offered to you on many occasions—so I don't understand why you're staying in a motel when it would be easier to stay at my place."

For the moment, Kelly remained quiet, but she didn't take her eyes off Joe. His tousled dark hair seemed to be sprouting more grey, especially around the temples. He was handsome in a rugged way, like someone who spent a lot of time outdoors, and she liked that about him. She wasn't into the baby-face type. He didn't have a beard, but he did have a mustache, which she thought added to his fortyish Tom Selleck look. "It's complicated," she finally said.

"How so?"

"I just think I'd feel awkward."

"Why?

"I don't know."

"Yes, you do," Joe wasn't going to let up. "Kelly, I know there's chemistry between us. You don't want to admit it, but it's there. We're both professionals and we're working on a very important case, and it takes precedence. I can separate the two and keep my business hat on, but maybe you're worried you can't. You know you can trust me. I know how you want things kept between us, and I'll respect that—at least for now," he said with a smile.

Kelly knew there was some truth to what Joe was saying. *Maybe I am more worried about keeping my own feelings in check. It does make sense to stay in his spare bedroom and it would save time, especially if we do have to take off at a moment's notice. Like he said, we're both professionals, and right now Sara is our focus.*

"I can also make a mean omelet and the best cup of coffee in town," Joe added, breaking the silence.

Kelly smiled. "Your offer is very tempting and deserves consideration."

The GPS went off. "In two miles, turn right," she announced. They turned onto a dirt road and were told to stay on that road for five miles, then make another right.

"This is really out in no-man's-land," observed Joe.

"Just the kind of place a kidnapper might want to take his captive," said Kelly. "Joe, I'm getting a good feeling about this place. We might be onto something." Just then, Joe's phone rang.

"It's Luke, he must have information or he wouldn't be calling yet."

Chapter Twenty-One

Sara didn't sleep well. Her mind was actively planning one escape scenario after another. Self-defense didn't work at the boutique, but her options were limited, and she'd have to try something. He was trusting her now and might let his guard down. If she could persuade him to take her outside for a few minutes to get some fresh air, her chances would be better.

She heard footsteps coming down the stairs and then the key in the lock. The door opened and he walked in, carrying a tray of food in one hand and the key in the other. He stuck the key in his right pocket and set the tray on the wooden chair.

"I made you something special this morning, scrambled eggs and bacon with a side of cantaloupe." Sara looked at the tray. Next to the paper plate of food was a plastic fork and spoon—no knife—and a plastic cup for water. No coffee, as usual—too hot, she suspected, and could be thrown in his eyes. He was careful to eliminate any possible threat.

"Thank you, Mister. You've been very kind to me," she said, trying to sound sincere. She had to keep up the act, including not knowing who he really was. She thought long and hard about whether or not to tell him that she knew he was Ross the waiter, but not knowing how he'd react, she feared losing what little trust she might've gained.

Sara went over to the plate and picked up a piece of bacon. She took a big bite and smiled at him. "This is just the way I like it, nice and crispy. Mister, you said you were planning something special for today," she said, looking at the plate of food. "I like how you started the day," she said, continuing to smile. "I enjoyed our picnic yesterday. I think it would be really special if we did something like that again, especially if I didn't have my wrists taped and my eyes weren't covered. Then I could appreciate the beauty of being outside. Were you thinking of something like that, or would you rather not tell me and surprise me when you're ready for me to know?" She wanted to plant the idea of being outside with no restraints, but then she moved on quickly so he wouldn't question her motive. She was playing the role of her life and hoped he'd believe the character she pretended to be. Sara was in survival mode. She had to try and hide the fear and disgust she felt every time he entered the room.

Before he spoke, he looked at her for what seemed like an eternity. "I have to leave for a while and take care of some business. There won't be a picnic. My surprise won't happen until tonight, but I need some information. It occurred to me that you need clothes—since you didn't have time to get any before coming here—but I don't know what size to get you." Sara felt the blood drain from her face when she considered what he may have planned for the evening. She had to say something, but the words wouldn't come. For a moment she was speechless, then she saw the trusting look in his eyes begin to change.

"Mister, that's very thoughtful of you, but I'm not used to someone buying clothes for me. I wouldn't know where to start. Most of my closet contains items that I take home from my boutique. Since they are individually made, the sizes aren't consistent with those in a department store. I just try on something I like, and if it fits, then it becomes mine." She kept her voice soft and genuine. He didn't say anything, but Sara could tell by the way his eyes were studying her, that he wasn't going to give up.

"I have an idea," she said. "Why don't you surprise me. I'm easy to please."

"I used to buy clothes for my wife on her birthday and other special occasions. She didn't always like them, but I always got the size right." He looked her over again. "I know what to do." Before leaving, he made clear what his intentions were.

"Sara, I'm planning on making a nice dinner for you. I want to bring you upstairs. We'll sit at the kitchen table." He rubbed his forehead with both hands. Sara wondered if he had a headache but thought it best to remain quiet. He continued. "I want to show you that I can be a nice person and I want you to trust me, but I'm having nightmares. In my dream, you start off being nice to me, then you see I can't move and you laugh at me and call me stupid. You turn into Betty and run out the door. I can't chase you because my legs won't work. Sara, something's going to happen tonight, and whether it's good or bad depends on you." He rubbed his head again.

"I've had nightmares and I know how upsetting they can be," she said, keeping her voice calm. She could tell he was becoming more fragile. "Sometimes, bad dreams are brought on by concerns that we have. I'm not Betty and I would never laugh at you or call you stupid."

"I want to believe that. I guess I'll know tonight." He kept rubbing his head and mumbling that it was hurting more and he couldn't think straight, and he had to leave before it got worse. "I have a lot to do so I have to go now."

"Thank you again for breakfast, it's very good," she said, taking a bite of the eggs while trying to force a smile. Instead of paying attention to what she was saying, he seemed focused on the pain in his head. He kept rubbing it and mumbling under his breathe.

He left, and she was relieved to hear him go up the stairs. She felt helpless and nauseous from all the pretense and went over to the mattress to lie down. Her chances of getting away were limited. She thought about her mother and their last conversation, and wondered where the police were and why they couldn't find her. Day three and her hopes of surviving were fading. She replayed everything that had happened since she'd been taken, right up to when he brought breakfast that morning, including every detail of what he said to her. She sat up and looked toward the door. Something was different. The sounds when he'd leave had been etched in her mind, but that morning there was one sound she didn't hear—the key turning in the lock.

Chapter Twenty-Two

Detective Reynolds sent Officers Thompson and Mackey in two separate unmarked squad cars to stake out the post office. If Ross showed up, Thompson would take the lead and follow him with Mackey a few cars behind. If Ross made a turn, Thompson would continue straight and Mackey would veer off and follow the white van as long as he could without Ross noticing.

An hour had passed with no unusual activity, then a white Ford Econoline pulled into a parking space. Mackey and Thompson were on their phones with each other when the van showed up. They watched as a tall muscular man stepped out of the vehicle. The shirt he wore didn't cover up the breaking heart tattoo with the snake going through it. The adrenaline was flowing in both officers when they knew without a doubt that it was Ross Chatfield—they had their man. Mackey could hardly contain himself. He wanted to arrest him on the spot, but he knew if he did, there'd be no hope of finding Sara. Ross would deny every-thing, and if Mackey took him in for questioning, precious time would be lost. They didn't have enough evidence to hold him. Their only hope was for Ross to lead them to Sara.

After a couple of minutes, Ross came out of the post office with a few envelopes in hand. Before getting into the van, he opened one of the envelopes, then hopped in and started the engine. Mackey called Detective Reynolds.

"He's pulling out now. Thompson's pulling out behind him. I'll stay a car length or two back from Thompson," Mackey told the detective.

"You're sure it's him?"

"Definitely. We saw the tattoo. Hold on, I think he's pulling into the bank's lot. Now he's going through the drive-thru. I see Thompson parking on the side street next to the bank. I'll hang on the opposite side at McDonald's." Mackey told the detective about Ross opening one of the envelopes before getting in the van.

"It could've been a check he was expecting from his parents. He probably went to the bank to cash it. Interesting that Sara isn't with him, unless he has her tied up in the back."

"I don't think she's in the van," said Mackey. "He never looked around to see if anyone was watching, and he never looked in the back of the van when he got out or when he got back in. He must've left her wherever they're staying."

"Mackey, call me back when you're on the road again and give me which direction he's headed. I'll contact Joe and Kelly, but I'll wait to hear from you first."

"Detective, he's coming out now. Thompson just pulled behind him and I'm not far behind Thompson. He passed the on-ramp to the highway and, for some reason, he's taking all the side roads. Where the hell is he going? Geez, now he's pulling into the mall's parking lot. Thompson's going around the block. I'll circle through the mall's lot to keep him in sight and see what he does."

Luke couldn't believe what he was hearing. "This creep has Sara stashed somewhere and he's going shopping?"

"Looks that way. He just parked and he's going inside."

"Okay, Mackey, get back to me when you're on the move again. In the meantime, I'll check in with Joe and Kelly and see how they're doing." He no sooner hung up from Mackey when his phone rang again. It was Kim. He wondered since Ross was gone if Sara might have gotten away and managed to get to a phone and call her mother.

"Hi, Kim, is everything okay?"

"I don't know, you tell me, Detective. I could hardly sleep last night wondering what was happening to my daughter. I know you're all busy trying to find her, but I couldn't wait any longer to talk to someone. Do you know any more than what you told me last night?"

Luke almost wished he hadn't answered the call. He didn't want to let Kim know that they were following Ross and get her hopes up. He wanted to wait until he knew where Sara was. "Kim, there's not much I can tell you at this time, except to say that we're following up on a promising lead. I'm leaving here shortly, but I'll be in touch as soon as I know something." He heard a sigh on the other end.

"Detective . . . Luke, will you please call me by this evening with *any* news—good or bad? I know I'm asking a lot, but I can't wait another day without knowing something. Sara's all I have. She's my daughter, my best friend, my everything."

Luke felt the emotion in her voice. "I understand, Kim. I promise that, either way, I'll call you tonight." He hung up and leaned back in his chair. He thought about Kim and Sara's relationship and again wondered if he'd had a child, would they have been as close as Sara and Kim. Or, would he have been an absentee father when his child needed him the most. Maybe Ruth was right, maybe it was best they didn't have kids.

Forty-five minutes passed before Mackey called the detective to let him know that they were on the move again. "Ross got on the highway a few miles past the mall," he said.

Luke walked to his car but stayed on the line with Mackey until he had a good idea of what direction Ross was driving. "I'm leaving now and I'll head that way. When traffic thins, stay far enough back so he can't make out your vehicle," said Luke. "We'll eventually find him. I'll call Joe and see if he and Kelly can join us." He hung up and immediately called Joe.

Chapter Twenty-Three

She quietly walked to the door, hoping if he was still there, he wouldn't hear her. After a few minutes, she gently turned the door knob. The door opened, and her heart started pounding. She wanted to run for her life, but she had to make sure he was gone. Little by little she opened the door until there was enough room for her to ease out. She gingerly took each stair step, pausing after each one to listen for any noise. When she got to the top of the stairs, she was in the foyer. Straight ahead was the living room, and to her left was the front door securely locked with deadbolts. The atmosphere was still, and Sara felt she was alone. Looking down the hall to her right, she saw the kitchen and cautiously went that way. The back door had a deadbolt at the top, that could be secured from the inside with a key, but it wasn't fastened, indicating that was the way he left. The doorknob was locked, but it could be opened from the inside—he obviously wasn't expecting that she'd be able to escape from the basement. Stepping out on the deck, she looked around the property but had no idea where she was. The fresh air felt good and she breathed it in. He said he had things to do that morning, and she hoped if he took time to buy her clothes, that he wouldn't be back for a while—giving her time to figure out the best course of action.

Maybe he has a landline in this place, she thought to herself. She went back inside hoping to find a phone somewhere. There wasn't a landline, but when she looked in one of the bedrooms, she spotted her cell phone on the nightstand. She grabbed it and headed for the back door. She wanted to get as far away from the house as possible and out of sight before calling her mother or the police. As she was leaving, she saw the butcher block on the counter and pulled the largest knife and took it with her.

Once outside, Sara walked around the house, assessing her options. She saw the narrow gravel road and remembered the sound of it when Ross brought her here. That option was quickly ruled out. The woods were the only choice left, and they were less frightening than running into him on the gravel road.

Being a marathon runner, Sara had the endurance to run long distances should she need to. She wasn't fast, but she did have a head start on Ross. She stared at the woods, and not knowing which way to go, she wasn't sure how that decision would play out. She took a deep breath and headed towards the right side of the forest, hoping to come upon a road more traveled than the gravel one Ross used. When she was out of sight of the Chatfield property, she reached in her pocket and took out her phone, anxious to call her mother and the police. The phone wouldn't come on: The battery hadn't been charged and it was dead. She leaned against a tree and cried. At the moment, she was free—she'd escaped—but no one knew where she was or how to find her.

She had no way of knowing that Kelly and Joe and the police were on their way.

But would they get to her before Ross?

Chapter Twenty-Four

"Hi, Luke, you got something?" Joe asked, hoping for a positive response.

Luke told him about Mackey's call and everything that had transpired since that morning. "I don't know what the guy was doing at the mall, but he's obviously confident that Sara's going nowhere," he said. "He must have her tied up or locked in a room somewhere. The fact that he's taking time to run errands shows me that he's not too concerned about her leaving. He's back on the road now, and Thompson and Mackey are close behind. What's happening on your end, Joe?"

Joe told him where they were and their lack of progress thus far. "Kelly and I are optimistic about the next stop. The place is far out, has lots of acreage, and it's been empty for a while. We're almost there."

"You may be onto something, Joe. I'm not too far behind Mackey and Thompson and we're headed in the same direction as you. Unless he makes another stop or changes directions, we should all be in the same vicinity. Hey, Joe, you got a gun?" asked Luke. "You might need it if Ross has an accomplice watching her."

"Yeah, I keep a pistol in the glove compartment." The GPS sounded, indicating two miles left. "Luke, we're almost there. I'll let you know if anything concrete turns up," said Joe, adding that the house was off the beaten path down a long, narrow gravel road.

"Look at this place," Kelly said when they pulled up in front. The house was old, but in pretty good condition on the outside—nothing a new coat of paint and a few shingles couldn't fix. "There's not another home in sight, and it's surrounded by more trees than I'd expected. This has to be the place."

"Kelly, you stay here while I check it out." He asked her to get his gun out of the glove compartment. "I don't think I'll need this, but I'll take it just in case."

"I'm not staying here!" she announced emphatically. "If someone else is in there, you have a better chance with me by your side. We're just a couple out for a drive and got lost. If anything seems suspicious, we ask for a short-cut to the highway, then leave and call Luke."

Joe had to admit it made sense and would look less suspicious. "Okay, partner, let's go."

The grounds surrounding the faded grey house were left natural—dirt, rocks, scrub brush, and tumbleweeds. The old wooden steps leading up to the front door needed attention. There wasn't a doorbell, so Joe knocked. The door had a small window midway up, but it was covered by a curtain. There were larger windows on each side of the door, and they were also covered. Joe knocked, waited, then knocked again. Kelly put her ear to the door, but she couldn't hear anything. Joe turned the knob, and as expected, it was locked.

"Let's go around back," Kelly suggested. The back of the house had a large deck. The only things on it were a

Weber grill and an old lawn chair. Kelly tried to see in the window to the right of the door, but the blinds were pulled.

"I don't think anyone's here," said Joe.

"But Sara could be tied up inside. We have to find a way in, even if that means breaking a window."

"Kelly, we don't know if Sara's here, or if she's ever been here. We're going on a hunch, that's all. What are you going to do if she's not here—break into every vacant house?"

Kelly sighed. "I see your point, but I have a strong feeling about this place. If I'm wrong, I'll pay for the window and hope I'm not arrested for breaking and entering."

"You're not going to leave this alone, are you?"

"No," she said, and folded her arms in a determined stance. "I'm not leaving here without seeing what's inside."

Joe shook his head. "Okay, Kelly, but before you break the window, let me see how strong the door is, maybe I can kick it in." Joe grabbed the doorknob and got ready to kick, but before he could, his hand turned the knob and the door opened. "I'll be dammed, it wasn't even locked." He pulled the gun from his ankle holster and they slowly walked in. It was eerily quiet inside, and the room was dark due to the windows being covered. Joe left the door open and they could see that they'd entered through the kitchen. Kelly found the light switch and flipped it on. Straight ahead was a refrigerator and to the right of it, the hallway. To the left of the refrigerator was a stove and counter top, which curved around to the sink. The room was neat and clean except for a dirty frying pan and plate in the sink.

"Looks like somebody's been staying here, but there's only one plate," said Joe. They headed down the hallway, passing two bedrooms and a bathroom—which also indicated that someone was staying there. The hallway led to the foyer and the front door. They saw the living room, then the stairs leading down to the basement. Kelly noticed several locks on the front door, all bolted and secured.

"That's odd," she said. "So many locks on the front door and the back door wasn't even locked." Joe mumbled something and headed down the stairs with Kelly close behind. They entered the dungeon where Sara was held prisoner. The light was on, but no one was there.

"Joe, someone's been here," Kelly said, walking over to the mattress. She noticed the paper plate and plastic fork. "This has to be the Chatfield home, and this must be where Ross is hiding Sara. But where is she?"

"He could've moved her elsewhere before he went on his errands."

"I don't think so. Every lock on the front door was in place, and yet the back door was unlocked. Somehow Sara must've gotten out of this room and left through the back. That would explain the door being unlocked."

"If that's true, where did she go? I don't think she would've gone towards the road for fear he'd come back and see her. This place is pretty isolated, and Sara most likely had no idea where she was."

"I know. If I were Sara, I would run through the woods, hoping to find a neighbor on the other side. I think that's probably what she did, but that might create another problem. If Ross hoped to see a deer or a wild boar when he stayed here, that wild boar would have to come out of those woods." Kelly and Joe looked at each other and headed for the back door. They stood on the deck, staring at the woods. There were trees to the left, straight ahead, and to the right of the house.

"Which direction do you think she would've gone?" asked Joe.

"I'm not sure. If it were me, I wouldn't go straight ahead, assuming that's what Ross would do."

"I agree."

"Joe, we might have a better chance of finding her if we separate and each go in a different direction."

"I think we'll have a better chance of not having a boar encounter if we stay together. Plus, I have a gun." Kelly looked at the gun.

"I don't know if that gun is capable of stopping an agitated aggressive wild boar, but I see your point." Joe put the gun away and reached for his phone.

"I'll call Luke and let him know what's going on, have him send more manpower. We'll start at the left side and have them work the middle and right. Not knowing how far the woods go, Sara could easily get disoriented, and there's no telling where she'll end up."

Joe gave Luke the location of the Chatfield property. Luke said they were headed that direction and that Mackey and Thompson were only a few minutes behind Ross. With all the stops Ross made, Luke was able to catch up to them.

"They'll be here shortly," Joe said, as he ended the call. "Come on, Kelly, let's go."

Chapter Twenty-Five

Now that Luke had the location, he told Thompson and Mackey to stay out of sight a few minutes longer, and then approach the premises. They parked a distance from the house so they wouldn't be heard, but by the time they got there, Ross was out of the van and in the house. Mackey and Thompson went to the front door, guns drawn, and Luke went around back. He cautiously approached the back door, but he didn't knock. Gun in hand, he slowly turned the handle and entered. There were bags on the table, but Ross was nowhere in sight. Luke figured he went to the front door to see who was knocking, then saw that the basement door was open. Luke heard Ross stomping up the stairs and positioned his weapon.

"Hands up! Hands up!" he yelled.

Ross was frantic. "What did you do with her? Where is she?"

"Get down on your knees and put your hands on your head!" Luke commanded. Ross charged at the detective as Mackey and Thompson rushed in and tackled him to the floor. In a matter of seconds, it was over. The handcuffs were placed without incident.

"I didn't do anything," Ross protested. "Sara wants to be with me. You can't do this. I have to find her. We had a special evening planned."

Thompson, equal in muscular build but two inches taller than Ross, got in his face. "You're delusional buddy! Maybe sitting in a cell will bring you to your senses."

"If anything happens to Sara," Luke said, "you'll be looking at a lot more than kidnapping. Thompson, take him in. I'll deal with him later."

"Detective, do you want me to stay, or go with Thompson?" asked Mackey.

"I wanted you to stay and help search, but this guy could be a handful, and Thompson might need you. We'll collect whatever evidence we need later, but I'm counting on finding Sara alive." Thompson led Ross to the squad car, and Luke told Mackey to try and get Ross to talk about Sara on the way back to the precinct. He hoped, in his confused state, that he might indicate if she'd been harmed.

Before entering the woods, Luke texted Joe and said if they didn't catch up with each other, that he and Kelly were to head back to the Chatfield house at dusk. He didn't know if they'd have reception, and if they did, it might be sporadic. But he felt a text would get through easier than a call. He wanted to make sure they were out of the woods before dark.

The woods were thick, but there was little underbrush. There were pinyon, juniper, and some taller pine trees throughout, but the forest wasn't difficult to maneuver. Luke picked up a fallen branch and pushed aside pine needles and cones along the way, hoping to find a sign that Sara had been there. He called out Sara's name over and over, hoping to get a response. It was exceptionally hot for the end of April, and the shade from the trees was welcomed.

Kelly and Joe stayed close to each other, separating only to cover more territory, but they were never out of each other's sight. The woods were quiet, except for an occasional bird chirping.

"Kelly," Joe said, "look straight ahead." He pointed to a deer in the distance, then he caught sight of a fawn walking up to the doe. Kelly saw it, too. She pulled out her phone and took a picture. "They're pretty far away," he said. "They may look like two spots in the picture."

"I can always edit and bring them up closer." She put the phone back and watched the fawn nuzzle up to her mother's face. Joe took notice.

"What are you thinking, Kelly?"

"The symbolism in watching the doe with her fawn—I want to remember this moment," she looked at Joe. "I hope we can bring Sara home to her mother." Kelly called out Sara's name and the deer moved on.

"At least we haven't heard or seen a wild boar," said Joe.

"I don't think we will this time of day. Boars are nocturnal animals, and they tend to be more active in the morning or late evening—with the exception of winter. Sometimes they can be more active in the middle of the day when they're hungry and looking for food."

Joe was impressed with Kelly's knowledge. "Since when did you become a scholar on boars?"

"Since I had a vision of them. I did some research to see just how aggressive they were, or could be, around people."

"And what did you find out?"

"They can be extremely aggressive, especially when they feel threatened. I think a female with piglets could be very dangerous. Usually, you won't see a male with a female. It seems once he impregnates her, he's off. The males live more of a solitary life." They talked some more as they searched, taking turns calling out Sara's name.

"We've covered a lot of territory, and I'm getting a sense Sara didn't come in this way," said Joe. "Let's move towards center."

"I don't think she came this way either. I would've started slightly right of center," said Kelly.

Joe looked puzzled. "Why didn't you say something when I suggested left?"

"I don't know. I had no concrete reason to argue your choice."

"When have you needed a concrete reason to act on your feelings?" Joe said, sounding annoyed that they might have wasted time when they should've been looking elsewhere.

"I didn't take time to think it through. I guess I was hoping you were right and we'd find her here. But I agree with you now. I don't feel she's in this area," she paused a moment and then continued. "Joe, maybe we're not supposed to find Sara."

"What do you mean by that? Are you saying Sara shouldn't be found?"

"No, that's not what I'm saying. I'm saying maybe it's not you and I who find her."

Joe looked concerned. "Kelly, do you think Sara will be found?"

"Yes."

"Alive?"

"I hope."

Chapter Twenty-Six

She didn't know where she was or where she should go, but Sara kept running, wanting to get as far away from him as she could. She ran in and out of trees, feeling at times like she was going in circles. The forest was dry, and occasionally she could hear pine needles crunch beneath her feet. She slowed to a walk and leaned against a tree to catch her breath. A fallen tree caught her eye and she went over to it and sat down, trying to get a sense of what she should do next. She noticed the knife still clutched in her hand. *I don't even remember taking this. I wish I'd thought about water instead, but maybe this will prove more useful,* she thought.

The woods had no clear path, and Sara's sense of direction was skewed. The sound of traffic was nil, and her hopes of hearing cars on a well-traveled road faded. She felt there might be neighbors on the other side of the woods, but she didn't know how to get to them. She thought about all the times she'd been hiking and never once did she get concerned about getting lost. But that was on trails frequented by other hikers; this was a predicament like none she'd ever experienced. Being kidnapped is not something you plan for. Her self-defense class didn't prepare her for what to do if you escape a kidnapper but have no idea where you are and no way of contacting anyone. Her situation was challenging, but Sara was not one to give up easily. As dire as things appeared, she'd rather take her chances starving to death in the woods then to be kept prisoner by a crazy man.

I have to stay calm and focused. Panicking will not help me survive.

Sara looked toward the sky to see the sun's position, then she glanced around the woods. There seemed to be more daylight coming from the west. Hoping it would lead her out, she decided to go that way.

Every hundred feet or so, Luke would call out Sara's name, but to no avail. He thought about Kim and how worried she must be, not knowing if they'd find Sara, and if they did, would she still be alive? Kim didn't know they were all in the woods looking for Sara, and wanting nothing more than to bring her home safely. She also didn't know that Ross was in custody.

Luke looked at his watch, surprised that so much time had elapsed. The woods weren't thinning out; if anything, they seemed to be getting thicker. He searched the ground closely for any sign that Sara might've come that way. He paid attention to his surroundings and marked trees along the way with the pocket knife his father had left him. After removing some bark, he numbered the trees starting with a straight line. When he came to the second tree to be marked, he made two straight lines, adding an extra line for each tree until he came to the fifth one. After making four straight lines, he ran a line through the fourth to equal five. He kept adding lines to each marked tree, making sure he hadn't gone too far before tagging another. Luke wasn't meticulous about most things, except when it came to work. He learned early in his career that lack of attention to detail could prove deadly. Paying attention to his surroundings and leaving a trail could prove beneficial. Not only would it make it easier to find his way out, but should he encounter problems, it would help others know which direction he took.

The sun had moved further west and Luke was getting concerned that Sara wouldn't be found before dusk. He came across a downed tree and sat to rest his legs. He couldn't understand why Sara hadn't heard him or Kelly and Joe calling out to her by now. *The woods can't be that large,* he thought. They had to be getting close. He told Joe and Kelly to start back before dusk and meet him at the house, but in his heart, he knew he wouldn't be going back without Sara. He didn't want to leave her alone in the woods all night. Kim had asked him to call that evening, no matter what the news, but would he be able to do that? Would he have reception? Still holding the branch he'd picked up, he leaned it against the tree to get his phone when something caught his eye. On the ground by his feet, he noticed some of the pine needles had been scattered, as if someone had sat there and shuffled them with their shoes. He knelt down to get a closer look. There was nothing definitive like a shoe print, but in his gut, he knew Sara had been there. He stood up and looked around.

"Sara! Sara!" he yelled, his voice louder and his pace faster.

Chapter Twenty-Seven

"**J**oe, we don't have much longer before we have to start back. I feel like we're looking for a needle in a haystack."

"I know. It feels hopeless, and yet we know she has to be here somewhere. We've been taking turns calling her name. Wouldn't you think, as still as it is, that our voices would carry and she'd hear us?"

"I don't know. I'm sure Luke is calling out to her too, and we don't hear him. But I have a feeling he's closer to where Sara is than we are." Joe gave her a look, but he didn't say anything. They continued searching and calling out Sara's name when, suddenly Joe stopped. "Kelly, I just thought about something. I've been calling Sara's name for the last hour because my voice is louder, and you felt it would carry farther than yours. What if Sara hears me, but she doesn't respond because she thinks it's Ross? She could be within hearing distance but is scared to death Ross is catching up to her."

Kelly took a deep breath and let it out slowly. "That's a good point. Let's clear our heads and try to imagine what Sara's thinking. She's been held captive for days, terrified of what Ross might do, and she's now running for her life not knowing if Ross is close behind. If I were in Sara's shoes, I don't think I'd be responding to a male voice either. Maybe I should be the one calling out to Sara . . . at least for a while, anyway."

"Sounds good to me," said Joe.

They continued on, and every so often Kelly would call Sara's name. Then something caught her attention. "Look at this, Joe," she said, pointing to a tree in front of her.

"Interesting. It looks like someone deliberately marked it. It's pretty deep, as if it was made with a knife."

"I don't think it would've been Sara," said Kelly. "We don't know if she has a knife with her, but even so, she wouldn't be leaving clues for Ross to see."

"That's true. Maybe Luke made it to mark the route he was taking."

"Sounds reasonable, considering the size of these woods."

"If he did, I'm sure we'll come across more signs like this," Joe said, looking around at all the trees. "Kelly, we covered a lot of territory on the left side. If by chance Sara went farther left than where we started, then we're way off base."

"I don't think she would've done that. The left side is closer to the house and she escaped through the back door. It would make sense for her to run straight ahead towards center, where we are now, then turn to the right once she's in the woods—provided she can think clearly enough to do that. It seems she'd have a better chance of running into a road or a neighbor's house if she continued right . . . but I could be way off."

Joe spotted another marked tree. "Look, Kelly, this one has two etched lines. I'm sure this is Luke's work. I wonder how far behind we are."

"Joe, you said that in the text Luke sent you, he mentioned there'd be a couple more officers coming. Did he indicate what area they'd be covering?"

"No, he didn't, but he did say they might not be able to join the search until morning. He could be marking the trees just in case they show up today, so they'd have an idea where he was headed. Either way, there's a good chance we'll catch up with one of them unless they head back to the house from another direction." Joe looked at his phone. "I hope Luke told them to bring a compass. I don't have any reception; we must be in the thick of it. If I'd known I'd be in the middle of the woods before I left this morning, I would've brought a compass."

Having different phone carriers, Kelly pulled hers out to see where she stood. "I don't seem to have reception either." She walked back and forth and then stopped. "When I move around, it goes up to one bar but then drops back again. I heard recently that a couple of new towers were placed in rural areas. If we're lucky, maybe one of them is located nearby and eventually we'll be in range."

After Kelly and Joe passed the tenth marked tree, they heard a faint sound in the distance and stopped to listen, but then it got quiet. Every few minutes, Kelly would holler Sara's name. Fifteen minutes passed, and then they heard something again.

"I don't know what that sound is, but it doesn't sound like a human voice," Joe said.

Kelly stood still, straining to hear. What she heard concerned her, and Joe could see it on her face. "That's not a human sound," she said, "that's an animal, or animals. They're waking up early. This is not good. We've got to find Sara before they do."

Chapter Twenty-Eight

Sara was thirsty, tired, and concerned she wasn't making progress. She felt so close to reaching open land, but she just couldn't seem to get there. Every so often, she'd take time to rest, but she was afraid to linger too long for fear Ross would catch up to her. She knew she had a head start, especially if he took time to shop, but she didn't know how well he knew the woods. She sat on the ground against a tree and tried to collect her thoughts. *Does Ross even know that I'm in the woods? Would he think I ran up the gravel road looking for a neighbor or a vehicle? Now that I think about it, that might have been the better choice. I think I would've had enough time to make it to the main road, but what if he'd forgotten something and come back to the house?* She sighed. *I can't over think this. I am where I am, and now I have to focus and figure out how best to get out of here.*

There was a noise in the distance and Sara felt panicked, wondering if it could be him. She stood and listened for footsteps. Where would she go if it was him? There was nowhere to hide, and she knew she couldn't outrun him. Staying calm was difficult, but if she panicked and lost control, he'd win. She held tight to the knife and walked slowly, afraid if she ran, she'd make too much noise. Each step was carefully taken to minimize the sound of dry pine needles beneath her feet. It wasn't long before she realized the sounds she was hearing weren't coming from Ross; she recognized the squeals and grunts from a hiker safety video she'd watched. A regular customer of Sara's—knowing she liked to hike—told her about an encounter her husband had had with a wild boar while hiking and recommended the video to her.

In all the years Sara had been a hiker, she never encountered an animal, let alone a wild boar. But she'd never been deep in the woods in an area where others didn't go. She stood still and listened, trying to figure out how far away the boars were and if they were coming in her direction. *It sounds like squeals from piglets, and the grunts I'm hearing have to be coming from at least one sow.*

Sara played the video over in her mind. She tried to recall the information she'd learned, but it had been a while since she'd watched it, and she wasn't sure how much of it she actually retained. At the time, she'd filed it away for a rainy day, but she never thought that day would come.

Wild boars are social animals and they like to live and feed in large groups that are comprised mainly of sows and piglets. However, there's usually one dominant male that hangs around. Sara thought about the sounds they make and remembered that they grunt for many different reasons, including communication, foraging for food, and sending a greeting to other boars to join their unit and feed with them. They liked to be in a unit of two or more. Sara could only hope that what she was hearing was one unit, and they'd go on by before others joined. She picked up her pace and walked faster, wanting to stay as far ahead of them as possible. Their squeals and grunts kept getting louder, but then she heard something that concerned her even more.

I must be losing my mind. Am I imagining things because I'm dehydrated? I'm hearing voices, and it sounds like my name, but that can't be. Does he know I'm here? Did he find me? Is that Ross? No, no . . . it can't be! I'm just confused. It must be coming from the animals.

The boars sounded like they were getting closer. Sara felt paralyzed; she wasn't sure which way to go. Her name seemed to be echoing off the trees, but it was coming from the opposite direction and she felt caught in the middle. Now she was convinced someone was saying her name. She heard it several times in a row, then nothing for a while, but each time she heard it, the voice got louder. She knew it had to be Ross. She didn't know what to fear more—a boar attack, or the voice. She began to run as far away from the voice as she could.

I may not survive a wild boar attack, but I'll take my chances. I like my odds better than being a victim of that maniac.

A loud, enthusiastic piglet squeal could be heard over the other boars. Soon Sara had the stranded piglet in sight, and she knew the sow wouldn't be far behind. She positioned the knife in front of her and held it between both hands. In reality, she knew the knife probably wouldn't be much help, especially if the male boar was present. The males defensively used their tusks to slash and stab, and they were very fast. The sows used their tusks to bite when in danger. If nothing else, the knife gave Sara confidence that it might help protect her from being bitten and give her a chance to get away. Soon the sow and another piglet appeared. Sara stood still and tried not to present a threat, hoping the sow and her piglets would move on. The sow made a noise and the stray piglet moved closer to her. Then the sow noticed Sara and made a different grunting sound. Sara knew what that grunt meant: It was a warning to the other boars that there was an immediate threat. Next came the growl—a sign of aggression—soon to be followed by an attack. The pig charged and Sara jumped aside as the video said to do. The growling got more intense and she charged again. Sara jumped to the side again, avoiding the sow just in time, but she knew she couldn't keep it up. The video also said to climb a tree higher than five feet. Sara quickly scanned the area for a tall tree that she'd be able to climb. She spotted one and ran towards it, and the sow charged after her. She jumped to the side one more time, using the extra few seconds to safely get up the tree. If you know what to do, you can prevent an attack, but only for so long, the video had said. The boar will wear you down if you don't get away.

Sara made it up the tree, anxious and scared. She was safe for now, but she wouldn't be able to stay up there forever.

Chapter Twenty-Nine

Kelly and Joe came across several numbered trees. "Luke must've come this way," said Joe. "If we continue on this path, we might meet up with him."

"Hopefully Sara will be with him," Kelly said. "We've got to be getting close. You'd think she would've heard one of us calling by now, unless she was afraid to respond."

"If she heard Luke or me, she might've thought it was Ross and kept quiet. I think if she heard you, she would've responded."

"I agree, but there's always the possibility she made it out and found a road or a neighbor."

"She could also be wandering around in circles," said Joe. "She's been traumatized and I'm sure she's scared and confused right now. And we don't know if she's been abused by Ross. There's no telling what condition she might be in when we find her—*if* we find her."

Kelly gave him a disappointing look. "Don't go there, Joe. We're on a rescue mission, not a recovery. I'm not going to let myself think the worst and neither should you."

"I'm just being realistic, Kelly, that's all. We don't know what we'll find, but I'll try to remain positive. I certainly haven't given up hope."

Kelly heard something. "Joe, do you hear that?"

Joe stood still and listened. It wasn't the animal sounds they'd heard earlier. Now they heard Sara's name being called. "That's got to be Luke. We can't be too far behind." Kelly and Joe took turns calling Sara's name, hoping Luke would hear them. Soon, they heard him switch from bellowing 'Sara' to yelling for Joe and Kelly. It was faint at first, but as they kept walking, his voice got clearer and louder. The closer they got to Luke's voice, they began to hear noises that could only be coming from wild boars, but they didn't sound as close to them as Luke did.

When they finally caught up with Luke, he was leaning against a tree waiting for them. They exchanged what little information they had about the area they'd covered and anything else worth noting. Kelly mentioned seeing the marked trees and Luke acknowledged that he had done that.

"I did it for a couple of reasons," he said, "not only in case I might need some guidance in leaving this place, but I thought if Sara came across one of the trees, she'd realize someone other than Ross was looking for her. Ross would be in a hurry to find her; he wouldn't be thinking about marking trees. Also, in case we need them, I have two guys joining us in the morning. Turns out they weren't available this afternoon. Geez, I think half the department's out with some kind of crud." Luke also told them about the fallen tree and how he felt Sara had been there. "I know we're getting close, but if we don't find her soon, we won't have enough daylight left to continue." Luke didn't mention that he wasn't leaving without her.

They walked in the same direction, but about ten feet apart from each other. Each took turns calling Sara's name. The further they went, the sounds of wild boars got louder.

"We're heading right towards those animals. Maybe we should go in a different direction and head away from them," said Joe.

Luke disagreed. "I think we need to continue the way we are, but if you and Kelly want to branch out, that's okay, too."

Joe looked at Kelly. "What do you think, Kelly?"

"I agree with Luke. I don't like what I'm hearing. The squeals and grunts have become more restless. The grunts sound agitated, like the pig is either cornered or has something or someone cornered. I don't have a good feeling about this. We have to continue towards the animals, and we have to hurry."

Chapter Thirty

Sara watched the pigs circling below. One false move and they'd have her. The knife wasn't much comfort, and even if she was able to get the knife in the sow, it wouldn't be enough to kill her. A wounded sow would be extremely dangerous. She was tired, exhausted, and thirsty. She wasn't sure how much longer she could stay in the tree. The branches weren't strong enough to hold her. She had one foot propped on a higher, sturdier branch and the other on a lower branch that didn't feel as secure. Both arms were wrapped around the trunk of the tree, which was supporting most of her weight. She heard someone calling her name and she could tell he was getting closer. At that moment, she feared both the sow and piglets and Ross. Either way, she knew her chances of surviving were slim.

I'm running out of strength, but I'm not giving up without a fight. And I think I'm hearing more voices. Is it my imagination? One sounds like a woman. Am I hallucinating?

Sara looked down at the sow and her piglets. She knew they could stay there for hours, much longer than she could last in the tree. Boars can run up to 30 mph, so trying to outrun one was pointless. Loud noises generally will scare them off, but there wasn't a way for Sara to make enough noise.

She tried yelling at them, but to no avail. In the distance she could hear other boars, and she was concerned they'd join the three at the bottom of the tree. Again, she heard her name being called. She heard a man, then a woman, and then she thought she heard another man's voice.

That can't be Ross—it's more than one person. Maybe it's the police. Sara got excited at the thought of being rescued. "Hello! Hello! I'm over here!" she yelled. Her voice was weak and she didn't know if she'd been heard. Her arms hurt and soon the knife fell from her hand, barely missing the sow.

"Sara! Sara!"

"Help! please help me!" she cried. Her leg on the higher branch cramped and she could feel her arms slipping. She hadn't slept well since being kidnapped and her stamina wasn't up to par. She'd been running and walking in the heat without water, and she didn't know how much longer she could hold on.

If you're out there and not my imagination, please hurry. "Help! Help!" she repeated, trying to muster up all the strength she could, hoping to be heard.

Luke was several feet in front of Kelly and Joe, and he heard Sara first. "Sara! Sara!" he yelled. He could hear her faint cry for help. "It's her, hurry up!" he shouted to Kelly and Joe, and he took off running. He saw the sow and the piglets first, then he saw Sara clinging to the tree.

"Sara, hang on. I'm here to help you!" He looked at the sow; she saw him coming towards her and growled. He knew what was coming next. All of a sudden a gun went off, and so did the pigs. He turned around and saw Joe holding his gun. Luke ran to Sara.

"I'm Detective Reynolds. You can come down now, you're safe."

"My leg's cramped and my hands and feet are numb. I might fall," she said weakly.

"I won't let you fall. I'll catch you. Sara, slowly work your way down, I'll be here."

Joe started to walk over and help, but Kelly stopped him. "Joe, let's stay back for a while unless Luke asks for our help." Joe nodded. He understood what Kelly meant. This was Luke's moment; he was the one to rescue Sara.

When Sara was almost down, Luke grabbed her and held onto her. She put her arms around his neck and cried uncontrollably, releasing all the emotions she'd harbored for the last few days. Luke wasn't an emotional man, but he fought back tears as he cradled Sara in his arms. Fatigued—emotionally and physically—Sara slumped to the ground, and so did Luke.

Kelly and Joe waited a little longer and then walked over. When Luke saw them, he smiled. "We did it," he said.

Sara looked up and Luke introduced her to Kelly and Joe. Kelly knelt down beside her. "Where's Ross? Is he out here somewhere?" she asked Kelly.

"Ross is in jail, Sara. You don't have to worry anymore about him. Sara, are you hurt? Did Ross harm you?"

"No, not physically." She was quiet a moment, and then asked if her mother was okay.

"She will be," said Luke. He stood up and helped Sara to her feet. "Sara, are you strong enough to walk? We'll help you."

She looked around the woods, and then at her rescuers. "Yes, I want to get out of here."

Luke smiled and held onto her arm. "You're going home, Sara. Your nightmare is over. You're going home."

Chapter Thirty-One

Luke wanted to take Sara to the hospital and make sure she was all right before taking her home—"home" meaning to Kim's house—but she assured him that she was okay, and all she needed was to see her mother.

"My phone is dead," she said. "Can I use yours to call my mom? I know she must be worried sick." As soon as she said it, she realized she'd never memorized any of the numbers that were programmed in her phone. "This is crazy, but I don't know my own mother's phone number. My phone was always with me, and there was never a reason to memorize it."

"These smart phones can be a blessing and a curse," said Luke. "I have her number on my phone. I promised her I'd call this evening with good or bad news." Luke could tell how exhausted Sara was from the horrible nightmare she'd been through, and he had a thought. "Sara, why don't I call your mother and let her know that I have some good news, and I'll be there shortly to share it with her. I don't know your mother well, but I think if you call her now, she'll overwhelm you with questions to make sure you're really okay. Why don't we surprise her and let her see for herself? It's going to be emotional for both of you, either way, but I think

"

when she sees you and can put her arms around you, she'll save some of those questions for another day. And this will give you a chance to rest before we get there."

Sara leaned back in the seat and smiled. "I like that idea, and I *do* know my mother. Once she hears my voice and knows I'm on my way, she won't want to hang up until she has me in her sight."

Luke made the call and then drove in silence, giving Sara her space. He had many questions of his own, but between Ross, the woods, and the wild pigs, Sara had been through enough, and his questions could wait another day. Sara was safe and Ross wasn't going anywhere.

When they arrived at Kim's house, Sara didn't immediately jump out of the car as Luke had expected her to do. Instead, she sat quietly for a moment. Luke studied her, wondering what she was feeling. He noticed a tear in the corner of her eye. She had her hand positioned to open the door, but she hesitated.

"Are you okay?"

She turned and looked at him and he could see the moisture in her eyes. "I think it's finally sinking in that I'm free from that maniac. I'm not going to be locked up again like a caged animal in a damp, windowless room. I never fully appreciated life before Ross. I thought I did, but I can see now how I took normalcy for granted," her voice quivered. "I don't know if I'll ever get that back. I don't know if I'll ever be able to trust again."

"It will take time, but eventually you will. You're a strong young woman, Sara, and you survived a horrendous ordeal when others might not have. Don't leave Ross with anything.

Don't give him the power to keep you from having the life you deserve." She slowly began to open the door, and Luke got out to go around and help.

"Hold on to my arm, Sara. Your legs might be a little unsteady." She took his arm and they walked up to the front door. When Kim saw Luke standing there with Sara, she almost collapsed with relief. She backed up to let them enter, but she could hardly contain herself. She stood in the doorway holding onto Sara—one minute crying, the next laughing with joy. Luke stood off to the side and watched the reunion.

"Sara, you're alive! You're okay! I was scared to death I'd never see you again."

"I know, Mom, me, too."

Kim looked over at Luke. "You did it. You found my daughter and brought her home to me. How can I ever thank you?"

"Your joy and gratitude are all the thanks I need. Kim, I didn't do this by myself. Joe and Kelly and two of my officers were involved in rescuing Sara." He looked at Sara and smiled. "And your resilient daughter played a huge part in her own rescue."

Kim walked Sara over to the sofa and then went to the kitchen to get her a glass of water. "Luke, can I get you anything?"

"No, thanks, I should be going. It's been a long day for all of us, especially Sara. You both just need time with each other right now. Sara, I'm sure you'll stay with your mom for a couple of days before returning to your home—at least I hope you will. What better place to rest up and heal?" he said, smiling at Kim. "Sara, I'll call midmorning and see how you're doing. I'd like to get a full statement from you as soon as possible so we can complete the paperwork on Ross and get things going on our end."

"Okay," she said.

"Kim, I wanted to take Sara to the hospital and have her seen by a doctor, but she was too anxious to get home and assured me that she was okay. She's been through a lot, and quite an ordeal today. She might feel more aches and pains in the morning. If anything seems worrisome, please encourage her to see a doctor."

"I definitely will," said Kim.

Luke started for the door, but Sara asked him to wait. She slowly got up and walked over to him. "I don't know what would've happened to me if you hadn't shown up when you did," she was on the verge of tears. "You literally saved my life. How do you thank someone for that?" she asked.

"Sara, don't underestimate your will to live, or your resourcefulness. You did everything you needed to do to give us time to reach you."

She put her arms around his waist and her head on his chest. "Thank you for being there for my mom. Thank you for not giving up on me."

Luke put his arms around her and rested his head on hers. His heart melted, and for the first time in his life, he felt like a proud parent.

On his way home, Luke was taken aback by how much this case had impacted him and how emotionally involved he'd gotten. He thought a lot about Kim and Sara, and again wondered if he'd had a daughter, if she would've been anything like Sara. He hoped so. He was impressed with Sara's strength and her tenderness. She was an exceptional young woman and, in his heart, he knew that she would be okay. His thoughts turned to Kim and what a loving and caring mother she was. He was envious of the relationship they shared, and he recognized the void he was feeling—the family he didn't have. As he drove, he found himself looking forward to seeing them again . . . even if it was only to get a statement from Sara.

Luke was tired, mentally exhausted and anxious to get home, but he couldn't get his mind off Kim. There was something about her he couldn't let go of, and he realized he wanted to see more of her. A smile came over his face.

Maybe.

Chapter Thirty-Two

This had been one of the more difficult cases Kelly and Joe had ever worked on together. They talked a lot about it on the drive back. Joe had worked a kidnapping case before, but Kelly never had.

"I thought helping to solve my best friend Tara's murder—and almost losing my own life in the process—was the most emotional and challenging thing I'd ever done, but working on this case has left me completely drained."

"It's been a tough case for sure, but Kelly, you were *meant* to do this."

"I don't know, Joe, being a journalist was much easier for me."

"That's because you were in your comfort zone. Journalism was all you knew and loved doing at that time. You're treading new water now, and you haven't reached a comfortable place yet, but you will."

Kelly had asked Joe to take her directly to the motel so she could pack up and check out. Joe was afraid she'd head straight back to Sedona once she did, and he didn't want that to happen. He had something on his mind that he'd been wanting to talk to her about, but he wasn't sure how she'd react, so he kept putting it off. He didn't want to put it off any longer. He needed to talk to her before she left Flagstaff.

"Kelly, when I drop you off, I'm going to run by the store and pick up a few items to make a light dinner. I was planning on you having dinner with me."

"That sounds good, Joe, but I'm tired, and I really should go home before it gets too late."

"It would be better for you to eat, relax, and rest up before you leave. And remember, I do have the guest room. Besides, I need to talk to you about something."

"'Need' sounds important. Are you sure you don't mean 'want'?"

"I feel the need to talk to you about something I want to discuss. How's that for an explanation?"

Kelly laughed. "Well, with that, how I can refuse? You've definitely sparked my interest and curiosity. But Joe, after roaming around in the woods all day, I'd like to freshen up before I check out and come to your place. You should be back from the store by then."

"Not only will I be back, but I might even have dinner ready," he teased. "It doesn't take long for cold cuts."

"Keep it light, Joe. Right now, I'm more interested in a glass of wine."

It was driving Kelly crazy trying to second-guess what Joe wanted to talk to her about. Did it have something to do with business, or was it personal? Did he want to talk to her again about moving to Flagstaff so she wouldn't have to make that drive every day? It made sense. Other than her friend, Gina, she didn't really have ties to Sedona, but she did enjoy living there, and she loved the area. With its beautiful red rock formations and the fantastic view of Bell Rock from her balcony, it was quite the contrast from Flagstaff. But Kelly did like all the forest that surrounded Flagstaff, and at an altitude of 7,000 feet, the temperature was more pleasant in the summer than most areas in Arizona. Kelly also enjoyed how visible the stars were at night. Flagstaff was the first international Dark Sky City, and being home to the Lowell Observatory, it made for some of the best stargazing in the country. But what if he wanted to talk to her about their relationship—or lack of—how would she react? Was she finally ready to let go of her fears and allow their relationship to develop into something more? Deep down in her heart, she knew, there was nothing she wanted more.

Joe met her at the door with a glass of champagne. "It's not wine, but I thought after the day we had—helping Luke find Sara, and knowing she's safe and out of harm's way— calls for champagne." Joe knew that if Kelly had her choice, she most likely would've chosen champagne over wine.

Kelly smiled and took the glass. "I'll take any excuse for a glass of champagne," she said, taking a sip. She noticed that Joe also had taken time to freshen up. He was wearing a burgundy shirt with the first couple of buttons open and khaki pants. She almost wished she hadn't agreed to dinner. He looked so handsome, and she wasn't at work in her safety net. "You clean up well," she teased.

"I couldn't let you get one up on me," he said, giving her a look of appreciation. "But of course, you did. Kelly, you look fantastic!" She was wearing slimming black slacks, a V-neck harvest green silk blouse, and black medium heels with a curved harvest green stripe running along the side of each shoe. She'd decided at the last minute to include the outfit when she packed for Flagstaff, on the chance that she and Joe would have dinner with Luke at a nice restaurant—at least, that's what she told herself.

"Anyone would look good to you after staring at trees all day," she said.

Joe laughed. "Come on, let's sit down." He led her over to the taupe leather sofa and they sat down behind a hardwood coffee table full of delicacies.

Kelly looked at the food and then at Joe. "I hope this is dinner," she said, noticing an array of her favorites, including smoked salmon, brie, white cheddar, and chilled shrimp.

Joe handed her a plate. "I didn't want to spend the evening cooking in the kitchen, and I know how much you enjoy appetizers—sometimes more than dinner. I also have a Caesar salad staying cold in the refrigerator."

"I think this will be plenty." Kelly sat back and closed her eyes for a moment. Then she took a bite of her brie and cracker and sipped her drink. They made small talk while they ate, then Joe got up to refill their glasses.

"Just half for me, Joe. I still have to drive to Sedona."

"Have I shown you the guest room?"

Kelly laughed. "You may have to if you don't get around to telling me what's on your mind."

"Another good reason to delay," he teased, handing her the glass of champagne.

"Seriously, Joe, what do you want to talk to me about?"

He sat down and set his glass on the table. "A couple of things. You may have an idea about one of them, but the second thing I want to talk to you about is even more important to me," he paused and looked into her eyes.

"Joe, I can't take the suspense much longer. Tell me what's on your mind."

"Kelly, I love working with you. We make a great team. I can't imagine coming to work and you not being there."

"I wasn't planning on going anywhere. I feel the same way, Joe."

"I know you do, but let me finish. Kelly, you're my partner in every sense of the word and I want to make it official. I want the business to be the Conrad and Murphy Agency—or the Murphy and Conrad Agency," he said with a smile. "You've earned it and you deserve it. I respect you and your insights more than you will ever know," he paused, giving her a chance to respond.

"I appreciate it, Joe, I really do, but I'm not sure. That could complicate things."

"How so? Are you concerned if you ever decide to leave, or you've had enough of me, that it will make it more difficult?"

Kelly took a sip of her champagne while she mulled over his comment. "To be honest with you, I can't imagine I'd ever want to leave. I still have a lot to learn, but I do believe I'm a quick learner."

"The best," he said, and took her hand. "The next thing I want to talk to you about is something I've been wanting to do for a long time." He continued looking into her eyes, but now he held onto both hands. Before saying anything else, he leaned towards her and kissed her on each cheek. "I don't know for sure how you feel, but I definitely know how I feel. Kelly, I'm in love with you, and I have been for a long time. I can't imagine life without you. Not only do I want you as my partner in business, but I want you to be my partner in life. Kelly, I love you and I want to marry you." He got down on one knee. "Kelly Murphy, will you marry me?"

Kelly felt her heart racing. She was speechless, overcome with emotion. She'd fought falling in love with Joe for such a long time. She didn't know exactly when it happened, but she knew she was in love with him too. The protective walls she'd built around her began to crumble.

Joe was concerned by her silence. "You don't have to answer right away, unless the answer is yes. I know you weren't expecting this, and I understand if you need some time."

Kelly put her hands on his face and pulled him towards her. "Joe, I'm scared to death right now, especially by what I'm going to say." She tenderly kissed him on the lips, and he responded by passionately kissing her back. She reciprocated.

"Does this mean yes?" he asked hopefully.

"A big, capital YES!"

Joe jumped to his feet. "This calls for more champagne," he said enthusiastically. "I'll get the bottle."

"Okay, but, if I have more champagne, then you should probably show me the guest room. I don't think I'll be driving to Sedona tonight," she said, seductively walking over to him.

He took her in his arms and kissed her. "I'd like to show you my bedroom first. It's on the way to the guest room. I'll let you decide where you want to sleep," he said with a wink.

Kelly smiled, "I don't think that will be a difficult decision."

THE END

Author's Note

The Man in the Photo: A Flagstaff Mystery completes the trilogy with my two favorite characters—private investigator, Joe Conrad, and journalist/private investigator, Kelly Murphy.

I've enjoyed writing about Kelly and Joe and I hate to see them go, but I know it's time to move on. As an intuitive writer, my characters prompt me to write and they let me know what they want said, and Kelly and Joe have made it clear that their story has been told.

My other works include *Only by Chance in Cripple Creek;* *Sedona's Deadly Secret;* and *Four Keys and a Cabin.*